D1272004

WEST GEORGIA REGIONAL LIBRARY SYSTEM
Neva Lomason Memorial Library

The Couple from Poitiers

The Couple from Poitiers

GEORGES SIMENON

Translated from the French by

EILEEN ELLENBOGEN

A Helen and Kurt Wolff Book
HARCOURT BRACE JOVANOVICH, PUBLISHERS
San Diego   New York   London

Copyright © 1946 by Librairie Gallimard
English translation copyright © 1985 by Georges Simenon
All rights reserved. No part of this publication
may be reproduced or transmitted in any form or
by any means, electronic or mechanical, including
photocopy, recording, or any information storage
and retrieval system, without permission in
writing from the publisher.
Requests for permission to make copies of any
part of the work should be mailed to: Permissions,
Harcourt Brace Jovanovich, Publishers, Orlando,
Florida 32887.

Library of Congress Cataloging in Publication Data
Simenon, Georges, 1903–
    The couple from Poitiers.

    Translation of: Les noces de Poitiers.
    "A Helen and Kurt Wolff book."
    I. Title.
PQ2637.I53N5813   1986   843'.912   85-24786
ISBN 0-15-122700-4

Printed in the United States of America
First edition
A B C D E

The Couple from Poitiers

I

Someone who had been speaking must suddenly have fallen silent. But within seconds Gérard had already forgotten who it was. It was even possible that no one had spoken. But if so, surely, he would not have been so struck by the change.

Needless to say, he had not been asleep. One does not fall asleep at a wedding reception, especially if it happens to be one's own. All the same, when, on leaving the room, the waiter – doubtless a reflex action – switched on the lights, Auvinet almost jumped out of his skin. Well, perhaps that was overstating the case a little. At all events, he gave a start, and stared about him, goggle-eyed.

It was as if he were no longer an actor, but a spectator. Or rather, he realized, with a sudden pang, his angle of vision had changed, and he was at once both actor and spectator.

Someone, he was almost sure, had suddenly ceased to speak, probably Monsieur Sacre. Someone, at any rate, who was given to uttering dreary platitudes, to which one paid scant attention, so that it might well take one a second or two to notice the silence.

The faint click of the switch, transmuting the cold white electric bulbs to a dingy yellow, made him abruptly conscious of the strange spectacle of a dozen people, all silent.

Occasionally, in a restaurant, when, for instance, one is looking for the lavatories, one goes through the wrong door, and there unexpectedly, one intrudes upon a wedding party. But to find oneself thus suddenly in the midst of a wedding party, when one is oneself the chief protagonist! Up to this moment, Gérard presumed, he must have been eating and drinking like everyone else, unaware of what he was doing.

Now, with sharpened perceptions, he was looking about him, observing every detail of the scene, down to the smallest specks of light and patches of shade, yet, in spite of this remarkable alertness, his head was beginning to swim.

To his left, against the wall, was one of those clocks with Westminster chimes, the kind poor families save up for years to acquire. He had known people, neighbours, who had shopped at the same grocer's for decades, a shop known for the inferior quality of its coffee, simply because they got gift vouchers with every purchase; and if they saved heaven knows how many hundreds of these, they could exchange them for a chiming clock.

The larger hand of this particular clock moved from three minutes to four to two minutes to four, and Gérard was already cringing in anticipation of the imminent striking of the hour.

Although this was December, it was not yet dark. The view from the window was of a section of road on which a misty drizzle was falling, and a block of buildings, flanked by a narrow cutting, at the end of which could be seen wet railway lines, and a solitary locomotive on the tracks, steaming, but to all appearances abandoned.

They would have done better to wait until it was quite dark before switching on the lights. The grey glimmer from outside and the yellowish glow of the electric lamps, instead of brightening the place, cancelled one another out, and merely added to the dinginess of the room. The patterned wallpaper took on a depressing, brownish tinge, and cracks and patches of damp were revealed in the corners. The ceiling, decorated with a scene painted in oils, was also much darkened, though naked figures, lovers perhaps, were still dimly discernible.

The most sinister object in the room, facing the table, so

that Gérard was looking straight into it, was a huge wall-mirror, somewhat speckled, with faint wavy ridges in the glass, which reflected the whole wedding party, a row of black backs surmounted by necks and hair, and another, opposite, of faces above stiff white shirt-fronts.

Someone had stopped speaking, there was no doubt about it, otherwise it would not have been possible to hear the ticking of the clock, sharp and crisp as the sound of a metronome, and resonating like a loud pulse in one's temples, until one could almost imagine that one was listening to the beat of a tom-tom. Was he the only one who had noticed? The others were bent over their plates. They were eating. A dish of lobster mayonnaise had just been passed round, and on each of the crude white pottery plates there were thick, congealed lumps of red and yellow.

In one and a half minutes' time the chiming clock would come to life. Only a quarter of an hour to go before Gérard and his wife were due to go upstairs to the room where their everyday clothes and their suitcases awaited them. Then the train. Then Paris.

He waited, rigid with tension, staring glassy-eyed into the aquarium-like mirror, in which, with a sudden shock, he found himself looking into the eyes of his wife, who was seated at his side.

Even in this meeting of glances there was something uncanny. It was as if she too had, for an instant, escaped from the wedding celebrations.

She was very close to him. He could feel her arm against his, her leg against his, but it was over there, in the mirror, that he caught the fleeting glimpse of uneasiness in her gaze. How long had she been watching him? She must have been expecting some response, a smile perhaps, or some other sign of recognition. Instead, in spite of himself, he continued to stare at her blankly, as if he had withdrawn into another world, where human feelings had no place.

Her nose, reflected in the mirror, was a little crooked. He

3

found this odd, never having noticed it before, and it altered her expression. From this viewpoint, her face had lost all trace of light-hearted vivacity. She was pale, with two bright red patches on her cheeks – and these looked anything but natural, rather as if she had rubbed her cheeks with a lobster. She was just a chit of a girl, like hundreds of others, rather sickly-looking, scarcely even pretty, or rather with the kind of surface prettiness that does not stand up to closer scrutiny.

Had he ever admired her looks? He had not the least idea. He preferred not to think about it. And yet presumably he had thought her pretty, seeing that, every evening for weeks on end, he had loitered outside the glove shop where she was employed as a salesgirl.

It was the smartest glove shop in Poitiers, double-fronted, with a lavish window-display of gloves of the very finest leather. The lighting spilled out in a golden disk on to the wet pavement. It had not always been raining, but it was the light shining on the wet pavement that remained in his memory.

It was always she, wearing a black silk dress, who, on the dot of six, began turning the handle that wound down the shutters. He always stood a little to one side. They exchanged nods. And always, no sooner had the window-lights been extinguished than she emerged almost at a run. They walked along like strangers until they reached the first turning, where they vanished into a dark little passage and at once linked arms, and then, in the shelter of a wall or a doorway, they exchanged kisses, mouth to mouth. This had been going on since the end of the previous winter.

At last, she was bending her head over her plate. She ate carefully, fearful of staining her white dress, the wedding dress borrowed from her eldest sister, and altered to fit her.

He was wearing a dinner jacket.

4

'You're making a big mistake, Gérard. You'd do better to order yourself an ordinary suit, black or even navy, that would be a useful addition to your wardrobe. . . .'

This was his mother speaking, needless to say. She too was there, reflected in the mirror, sitting next to Linette. She too was eating, daintily taking little bites off the end of her fork, wearing a fixed, forced smile, for the sake of appearances, even when no one was looking at her. This, however, in no way detracted from her air of martyrdom.

'In your circumstances, a white wedding is inappropriate. What's the point of throwing dust into people's eyes? It's just wasting money that ought to be kept for when it's needed. The same goes for this idiotic notion of going to a restaurant for the wedding reception! Why ever not have it at home, where the food is better and a lot cheaper. . . ?'

What would she have said had she known that he was paying half the cost of the meal? She had spelled it out to him very clearly: the bridegroom is expected to pay only for the church service and the transport; the responsibility for the reception rests with the bride's parents.

The dinner jacket was not new. He had bought it from the chief clerk at the office. He had told his mother that it had cost him two hundred and fifty francs, and she considered that he had paid too much. In fact, he had paid four hundred francs. Or rather, he had paid two hundred francs on account, and still owed the rest, having given his word to pay the balance by money-order in a month's time.

'Promise me, Mother, that you won't make a scene, or burst into tears, or say anything unpleasant. . . .'

That had been this morning, at home, in their three-room flat above Madame Doré. He had cut himself shaving. Large basins of water stood on the kitchen range, for him to wash in. She snivelled. She was not crying, but was obviously on the verge of tears.

'Do make an effort to be civil. . . .'

5

'What about them? When have they ever been civil to me? When have I ever had so much as a friendly word from them?'

'You know very well, you were the one who began it. . . .'

'When I consider that you are barely twenty . . .'

She too was in the middle of dressing. She was coming and going, wearing only her corselet. She was quite without modesty, where he was concerned. He could do no more than look away every time he caught a glimpse of her starkly white, flaccid breasts escaping from the loose-fitting garment.

'Sometimes I ask myself . . .'

'Oh! do shut up, Mother!'

'I know the subject embarrasses you. . . .'

It made him bristle, it stabbed him to the heart, in the end it goaded him into such a rage that one night, the night when he had announced his intention of getting married, he had come very close to striking his mother.

What business had she to subject him to that piercing, mistrustful scrutiny? She didn't know Linette. She had never even set eyes on her. But that did not prevent her from saying, 'No decent girl would throw herself at a man, without even having met his family!'

She went on saying it, but it was not so much what she said that riled him as the way she looked. In her expression he could read the suspicion that she had not the courage to put into words, but which she never stopped hinting at.

'Take it from me, it's your cousin Bertrand all over again. . . .'

The meaning of this, in his family, was unequivocal. For his cousin Bertrand, who was a medical student and therefore in a position to make a good match, had instead been forced to marry a little factory-girl who had been carrying his child.

This very morning, in the car on the way to the

6

Mairie. . . . It had been raining. The window would not close, and it was damp inside. A little shining droplet hung from the tip of his mother's nose, and her hands were cold inside her black cotton gloves. It was the last time they would be alone together that day. In a few minutes they would cease to be just a mother and son on their own. Henceforth, there would be a third person standing between them.

'Are you really sure, Gérard, that this marriage is going to make you happy? We were so cosy together, just the two of us.'

She was close to tears. She was weeping. He had to urge her to powder her nose before they went into the *Mairie*, and even when they went in she was still snivelling.

The tightening of coiled springs. They were all conscious of it, they felt it, they waited for it, interminably it seemed, and then at last the famous chimes were unleashed. Someone, Monsieur Coutant, stood up solemnly, drew a gold watch from his waistcoat pocket, wound it with deliberation, and announced, like a judge pronouncing sentence, 'Four o'clock!'

Linette murmured, 'It'll soon be time.'

And, God knows why, she felt moved to lay her hand on her husband's arm. Taking possession of him, perhaps? Madame Auvinet had always maintained that Linette was the one who had made all the running, and that her whole family had been determined to 'ensnare' him.

'People with three daughters, who can't wait to get them off their hands.'

And here was Gérard, suddenly seized with panic. Not that he was in agreement with his mother, exactly. In fact he knew that most of what she said was untrue. After all, he knew the Bonfils, and had been made welcome in their home. They were thoroughly decent people, a shade common, perhaps, but then they came from a different background. Their little house, with its large garden, in one

7

of the poorer districts of the town, resembled a workman's cottage. Linette's father was proud of having been employed by the railways for thirty years, and of having worked his way up early in his career to the position of head of the local train services. In his eyes, the railway network constituted a world apart, inaccessible to ordinary mortals, and he spoke of it with the solemn reticence usually accorded to state secrets.

He smoked a pipe with a long staghorn stem, which made a revolting gurgling sound as he sucked in his very potent, evil-smelling tobacco. Tufts of black hair protruded from his nostrils. He spent every free moment of his time working in his garden, wearing wooden clogs.

His wife, today, was dressed in black silk, with a large cameo brooch at her throat. No doubt as a result of some skin disease, her nose was very red, a rather startling feature at first glance, but Gérard had grown used to it. But why on earth had she powdered her nose so lavishly today, turning it from red to an even more unnatural violet, like some kind of boiled sweet? It made her look like a sad-faced clown. It was distressing.

Linette was rubbing her foot against his nervously. She glanced anxiously at the clock, and whispered in his ear, 'You really ought to ask the waiter to hurry things up a bit, or at least get him to pour the champagne for the toasts.'

Ah! yes. His mind had been wandering. He had completely forgotten about the champagne and the toasts. No doubt they would be Monsieur Sacre's responsibility. He was the assistant stationmaster, who had graciously accepted Linette's invitation to act as her sponsor. He was a person of some standing. One could feel it. His wife, a small dark woman with bad teeth, was wearing her fur coat slung over her shoulders, claiming that the room was cold. By this ploy, she believed that she was cutting a figure as a woman of the world, accustomed to high society, stranded in the company of nonentities.

8

And then there was Monsieur Coutant, with his air of a Jesuit in civilian dress, vying for position with the assistant stationmaster, for he held a power of attorney for Bonté, a firm of solicitors. There was also Madame Coutant, who was eating nothing. There was Mimi, Linette's sister, aged sixteen, who was a salesgirl at a branch of the Prisunic. She was wearing a pale blue satin dress, made to measure, which was rather stiff, and too voluminous for her skinny little figure.

'Waiter!'

The waiter, taking the hint, uncorked the champagne, with everyone's eyes upon him, watching eagerly for the cork to hit the ceiling.

'My dear friends, it is my pride and pleasure to raise my glass. . . .'

Outside it was still not quite dark. A sort of mist, the same colour as the mirror, blurred the glass of the windows, through which, on the other side of the road, the rectangle of a lighted window could be seen, and, in the room beyond, the bent figure of a woman working at a sewing machine.

'This young couple, setting out for Paris, to take their first steps towards . . .'

He must have clinked glasses with Linette, and then with all the family and guests.

'Well now, isn't it time you kissed the bride, young man?'

He looked at his wife. She came towards him. He kissed her.

'You can do better than that, surely?'

There were carnations on the white cloth, from end to end of the table. Gérard had stuck one in his buttonhole, as had his father-in-law.

In less than an hour the train would be bearing them off to Paris, and there would just be the two of them on their own.

His mother's expression was anguished, his mother whom he was about to leave alone in their midst. If only he could be sure that there would be no unpleasantness, that nothing regrettable would be said! She would leave, walking on the inside of the pavement towards their flat, to find everything topsy-turvy, as they had left it that morning.

'Shall we go up?'

He nodded, and made his excuses to the guests. They must not miss their train. . . . The guests watched them walking to the door. They mounted the staircase, with its reddish carpet and three missing stair-rods.

'What was the matter with you just now, Gérard?'

'Me?'

'You didn't seem quite yourself. I bet it's because you had too much to drink.'

'No. A little, perhaps.'

It was true. Abstractedly, he had drunk a good deal in the course of the day, but he was not drunk. On the contrary, he was all too chillingly alert, like a man awakening from a long sleep, or over-stimulated by an evening spent in a crowd.

They went into a bedroom. Madame Bonfils, a little intimidated, called up from downstairs, 'Do you need me, Linette?'

'No thanks, Mum.'

And when the door was shut, 'Poor mother! What will she think of next! Would you help unhook my dress? Your hands aren't greasy, I hope.'

He undid the hooks. She began changing her clothes. The only light was a dim, unshaded bulb dangling from a flex. There was nothing else in the room but a bed covered in a coarse red eiderdown and a little washstand with an enamel bidet underneath.

'We haven't much time.'

He changed his shoes. He had been wearing house-slippers, because they were cheaper than patent-leather pumps.

'Right up to the last minute, I was scared on account of your mother. I just hope she doesn't take advantage of our departure to make a scene.'

'I don't think she will. She promised me. . . .'

'Do you really think she knows?'

'She has her suspicions, but even if it wasn't true, she'd still believe it was. Where I'm concerned, she always thinks the worst.'

'How she must hate me! When there was no way of avoiding kissing me in the vestry, I really thought she was going to bite me! You can't imagine what an effort it was for me to call her "Mother".'

'Well, she is going to be left entirely on her own.'

'Still, she couldn't expect to hang on to you for the rest of her life.'

A silence fell between them. They went on dressing. Linette was changing her stockings.

'You didn't let it worry you too much, I hope?'

'No. All the same, it will be a relief once we've really got away. Especially on account of my sister. It's difficult when one is sharing a bedroom . . . and she was always watching me while I was getting dressed. . . .'

He said, almost tenderly, but not quite, because there simply wasn't time, 'My poor pet . . .'

And his thoughts reverted to that time, a month ago, when, shortly after he had collected her from the glove shop, and they were walking hurriedly through the dimly-lighted streets. . . .

'Can you be sure we won't run into anyone? Are you quite sure *he* won't tell?'

'He hasn't the right. Anything concerning a patient is a professional secret, according to medical ethics.'

'I'm so scared, Gérard.'

He could have taken her to see another doctor, a stranger. Why had he chosen to go to his family doctor, the one who had attended his father in his last illness, and whose patient he himself had been for as long as he could remember? They had been kept waiting a long time in the tiny ante-room, where there were a few old magazines scattered about. The doctor, without so much as a word of greeting, had ushered them into his consulting room. It was as if he had known all along what they had come about. Eventually, he had got around to asking a few questions, particularly about dates. Finally, under the harsh glare of an overhead light, he had subjected her to a hateful examination.

Then, straightening up, he had said: 'It's as you suspected, Mademoiselle.'

This pronouncement gave Gérard the courage to intervene.

'Look doctor. You know my mother. You're aware of my situation. Wouldn't it be possible. . . ?'

'No.'

'But couldn't you at least recommend someone?'

He had nothing to suggest. The only choice left to them was the small ads on the back page of the local paper. An old dirty house. A staircase with children at play, sitting on the steps. A smell of cooking. A hard-faced, grey-haired woman, who stood rubbing her chapped hands together as she listened.

'You must understand that two thousand francs is my lowest charge. There are too many risks. Only last week they arrested . . .'

He knew all too well that he could never scrape together two thousand francs. He owed money everywhere, even to the waiter in the café near the Pont-Neuf! He also knew that his employer, the notary Monsieur Malterre, wouldn't lend him a centime. Even so, he had plucked up his courage, and called on him out of office hours. It had been the first time he had even set foot in his flat. He had confessed everything.

'I'm very sorry, my dear boy.'

Had he not even gone so far as to threaten to take his life? Maybe he had, but he did not want to remember. That same evening he and Linette had roamed the streets interminably, she clinging to his arm, drooping a little with fatigue.

'As long as I'm only earning eight hundred francs a month, your parents will never give their consent. . . .'

The alternative was to leave things as they were, and remain in Poitiers. In that event, what possible hope was there of concealing the truth?

'Have you got the key of the suitcase?'

'It must be on the bedside table. Don't shut it yet. You've left my slippers out.'

He paced up and down the room, with a feeling that nothing was quite real. Perhaps she had been right after all. He probably had had rather too much to drink. He was feeling decidedly queasy and somewhat lightheaded. A deep wave of melancholy swept over him.

'Gérard . . .'

'Yes?'

She was gazing into his eyes. She was saying, 'There are just the two of us now.'

'Yes, my love, just the two of us.'

And he held her for a moment in his arms, dressed as she now was in her brown wool coat, with a little black hat on her head.

It wasn't that he was not fond of her, but it was all wrong, somehow. He was barely twenty. His mother had been right. He felt as if he were not so much leaving of his own accord as being thrown out, and he had not the least idea where he was going.

His mother could always sense it when he got himself embroiled in a pack of lies. And yet, he was a fluent liar. When there was something he badly wanted, nothing could stop him.

He had chosen to go to Paris because he felt he had to, because there was no longer any alternative.

He had always wanted to go to Paris, but not like this. He had always known that he could not spend the rest of his life in Poitiers, following in his father's footsteps, eking out his existence as a clerk in a notary's office.

He had always dreaded solitude. He had always wanted to join his life to another's. A couple. Even at the age of

13

eighteen, no! before that, whenever he had come upon two shadowy figures clinging together in the shelter of a doorway, he had been stricken with a sense of urgency, a sense of urgency that was almost akin to anguish. And when, later, he and Linette had trailed endlessly through the streets, stopping only to melt into the shadows of a dark corner, they had already found a window, a window always blazing with light in a dark street, their window, into which they gazed with longing.

They day-dreamed: A place of their own, just the two of them. Shutting the door behind them. Pulling down the blind. The two of them by lamplight, in a warm, cosy room.

'We'd better be going.'

The porter was already waiting on the threshold to carry down the two suitcases, one of them new, bought the previous day especially for the occasion. More debts. Was there anyone to whom Gérard did not owe money?

Downstairs the men were talking about them, lolling back in their chairs, smoking cigars with the bands left on. They were discussing the young couple's future prospects, the prestigious job that awaited him in Paris.

For was he not about to become a sort of private secretary to the novelist Jean Sabin, with a starting salary of two thousand francs a month? So glowing were his prospects that they were a source of some slight vexation to Monsieur Bonfils, who, after thirty years' service with the railways, was still earning only eighteen hundred. Monsieur Bonfils, though impressed, was secretly a little envious.

'On the other hand, we haven't the security of a retirement pension to look forward to,' he demurred, as a sop to his father-in-law's self-esteem.

And to think that it was all a pack of lies! Linette knew how matters really stood. They had discussed it, and fixed on a figure likely to persuade her parents to give their consent. In fact, Gérard was to be paid eight hundred francs, the same as in Poitiers – and out of that he had undertaken to send three hundred to his mother!

'Please, no! We don't want you to see us off at the station, it would only break up the party, isn't that so, Gérard? After all, it's only across the street. . . .'

She kissed her father and mother. Her farewell kiss to her sister lasted a little longer. Mimi whispered something in her ear, which made her laugh.

'Goodbye, Mother.'

'Goodbye, my son.'

Madame Auvinet was not doing too badly. She wasn't crying, just snivelling a little, and looking about her with a sorrowful expression.

'Look after yourselves.'

They shook hands with Monsieur Coutant and Monsieur Sacre. Then they went on their way. Now they were out of doors in the dark. It was still drizzling, and tiny droplets of rain clung to the wool of their coats.

'Have you got the travel voucher?' He had. They were travelling first class, since they had been able to get travel vouchers free. They were followed by the porter, carrying their bags. They crossed the station concourse, and made their way along the platform, where crowds of waiting passengers were strung out from end to end. It was cold and damp.

'Passengers for Paris. . . .'

The loud-speakers reverberated hollowly all over the station. A train loomed in the distance. Reddish sparks flew about all along the tracks in the damp night. Then a tremendous racket.

He helped his wife up the step, and handed her the two suitcases.

'Any seats?'

A red carpet. It was the first time either of them had ever travelled first class. They found a compartment with two people already in it, people from Bordeaux, businessmen probably, or lawyers, acquaintances anyway, since they were discussing personal matters while smoking. They were wearing pigskin gloves and, sitting as they were with legs crossed, their highly polished shoes and silk socks were much in evidence.

'I hope the smoke doesn't bother you, Madame?'

'Not at all, Monsieur.'

They continued their conversation, perfectly at ease, the aroma of the liqueur brandy which they had doubtless been drinking in the restaurant car still faintly detectable. A woman in mink passed by. She glanced at them casually, a little surprised, perhaps, by Linette's coat.

Gérard was painfully conscious of their deficiencies. He sensed that everyone had sized them up, even the steward who came round to distribute tickets for the first and second sittings in the dining car.

'You're very flushed', remarked Linette, having been watching him for some little time.

'Oh! It's very hot in here.'

'I can't help wondering if your mother . . .'

He had ceased to think about her. In three and a half hours they would be in Paris, the pair of them. Both clambering down on to the platform, and then taking the Metro.

Madame Bonfils had remarked to Madame Coutant, 'It's better for them to stay in a hotel to begin with. Flats are so hard to come by in Paris! It's as well to start by getting to know the town, and finding out what district suits them best. It will probably take them several months to get something they like. Then, once they're settled in, we'll send on their furniture.'

In the restaurant car, as he was opening the bottle of Listrac that was already on the table, Linette said warningly, 'Don't drink too much, Gérard. Your eyes are watering already.'

He could feel it. His eyelids were itching. He drank nevertheless, absentmindedly. It made him feel drowsy. In the corridor, he stood still for a while, and looked out through the slanting rain at the lights flashing past in the dark.

And each one of those lights seemed to him a kind of beacon. They passed close to a low farm-building, the roof of which barely reached above the embankment. Lights showed in two of the windows, and this in itself was enough to awaken a pang of envy in him. Even the sight of a small station, deserted except for a solitary employee on the platform, filled him with envy.

It seemed to him that everyone but himself had a place to go to, a warm, cosy, intimate little haven, and the throbbing rhythm of the train reverberated in his head, carrying him farther, ever farther into the unknown.

'You're very silent.'

He looked at their two fellow-passengers, who were still deep in conversation, sparing them no more than an occasional, casual glance.

If only he and Linette could have had a compartment to themselves. Then, perhaps, he could have lost himself, clasped in her arms. With all lights switched off but the blue night-light, they would have raised the blind and watched the dark landscape rushing by in the night, lit only by the occasional lighthouse beam, or the headlights of cars in the far distance, or the lamp of a cyclist waiting for the barriers to rise at a level crossing.

They were standing together out in the corridor, when they saw the first tall buildings of the suburbs of Paris, some standing quite alone, eight floors built of brand-new stone, with lights showing in every window, among the old-fashioned cottages, with their front porches and tiny gardens.

He felt an icy, ungloved hand slip into his. He squeezed it with unintended force, and, as the other passengers were putting on their coats and taking their luggage down from the racks, he heard Linette's voice murmur in his ear, 'There's nothing to be afraid of. You'll see!'

II

He wrote: 'You complain of loneliness, and reproach me for not writing often enough. If only you realized how little time one gets for leisure in Paris, especially if one is young, and still has one's way to make in the world. Living, as you do, in a remote backwater, it's hard for you to visualize Paris as the truly awesome battleground that it is. From the highest to the lowest, everyone is obsessed with elbowing his way to the top, and the devil take the hindmost. There's no time to give a thought to those who fall by the wayside. . . .'

He started, fancying he heard someone opening the door. Hastily, he slid the letter under his blotter, and replaced it with a packet of bluish envelopes, which he began addressing, taking the names from a printed list. But it had been a false alarm. There was no one there. Besides, he could hear the Major's voice talking to a visitor in his office upstairs.

There were times, towards the late afternoon, when Gérard would regress to his schooldays, when, as a small boy, lulled by the lamplight and the heat, he would grow more and more drowsy, though never quite dropping off to sleep, until the outlines of everyday objects became blurred and mysteriously shadowy, as in a world of dreams.

The table at which he was seated was an ordinary kitchen table, covered in brown paper secured with drawing pins, and already he had found time to scribble all over it, so that it was defaced with squiggles and initials.

18

At another table nearby sat Mademoiselle Berthe, plump and fresh-faced, her hair always neatly brushed, always smiling and unruffled, typing letters dictated by the Major. There, in the middle of the wall facing him, was a narrow black fireplace, with logs blazing in the grate. Drouin – in fact he always thought of him and addressed him as Monsieur Drouin – stood with his back to the fire. He was powerfully built, with the ruddy complexion of a Norman peasant, intensified perhaps by the heat of the fire. Drouin might almost be regarded as the boss. Certainly he was the man in charge of this office. He too had time to kill, and also spent it writing letters, which he slipped under his blotter whenever the Major put in an appearance. As he wrote, he wore a sentimental smile, which contrasted oddly with his powerful, bony features. Everyone knew that these letters were addressed to his mistress. Finally, on the wall to the right of Gérard's desk were two shutterless, uncurtained windows, two black, steamed-up rectangles at night, and the dark mahogany telephone switchboard, with its little white discs, dropping every time a call came through, its red plugs and its nickel-plated switches. And, close to the switchboard, pale and anxious-looking, sat Mademoiselle Lange, who really *was* Jean Sabin's private secretary, typing away at tremendous speed.

It was an old house at the end of a dark cul-de-sac, a barely noticeable passageway between two large buildings, one in the Rue Daru, the other at the far end of the Faubourg Saint-Honoré, a few yards from the Place des Ternes. Their own building had every appearance of having been left vacant for a long time. The printed wallpaper, having faded to such an extent that neither colour nor pattern was any longer discernible, was peeling away from the walls. The doors, once painted grey, were grimy, and the floorboards stripped of polish. Even the old gas-light fittings had been left where they were.

He went back to his letter, his head swimming, and endeavoured to recapture his train of thought.

'But I am not one of those who have fallen by the wayside, and I have no intention of doing so. I mean to succeed, and I will, and it's because I have always had this feeling that my destiny lay here that I made up my mind to leave Poitiers. Don't imagine, my poor dear mother, that I don't realize that this has caused you much distress. I know how lonely life must be for you, with so little to brighten it up. But, would it have been right for me to jeopardize my future? Surely you will be the first to rejoice in my success, when it comes, knowing that I owe it all to your sacrifices?

'Better times are on the way, you'll see. My determination is fixed. Here, I feel it with all my heart, there is a future for me, and, given time, I shall prove myself someone to be reckoned with. And Linette, whom unfortunately you never really got to know, will be a great help to me, because she has confidence in me, and is in sympathy with my ambitions.

'In the meantime, we live frugally, for one must look to the future. We deny ourselves all but the barest necessities, but even so you can't imagine how my wages just melt away. That's why I haven't yet been able to send you the money I promised you. Be patient a little while longer, I beg you. . . .'

It was half-past four. On the chimney-piece stood a box waiting to be filled with the day's outgoing mail. Shortly, at five o'clock, Gérard would empty it of all the letters, parcels and registered packets, and would take them to the post office in the Rue Balzac. Unless . . .

One of the metal discs on the switchboard fell down. Mademoiselle Lange picked up the receiver. The resonant voice of Jean Sabin could be heard through the amplifier.

'Is that you, Lange? Put me on to the President of the Council right away. . . .'

Mademoiselle Berthe, who had also got the gist, though not all the actual words were quite audible, turned towards Auvinet with a pleasant smile.

'What did I tell you? I bet this means the grand tour for you!'

After the President's office, it was the turn of the President of the Chamber of Deputies. Mademoiselle Lange announced, 'Monsieur Jean Sabin wishes to speak to . . .'

Then they all sat staring at the round white disc. These calls were always interminable. Jean Sabin, in his grandiloquent manner, was given to delivering entire lectures over the telephone.

At last, but now using his normal voice, he called from the bottom of the stairs, 'Lange! Come here, will you!'

She returned a few minutes later, typed out a press release, and handed a copy to Mademoiselle Berthe, who in her turn made a number of further copies.

'You'd better go and get a taxi, Monsieur Auvinet. It's the grand tour. And everything must be delivered by six o'clock.'

He already knew the routine. He put on his fawn raincoat, grabbed his hat, ran all the way to the Avenue Hoche, and had the good fortune to find Désiré's taxi at the head of the queue.

'The grand tour, is it?'

When he got back to the office, leaving the taxi waiting at the door, he found Mademoiselle Lange, who was expert at forging the signature of the Big White Chief, writing in cramped capital letters at the top of each envelope:

'URGENT. COMMUNICATION FROM JEAN SABIN.'

'I'll see to the post,' announced Mademoiselle Berthe. 'Are there enough stamps left?'

Abruptly, he concluded his letter to his mother:

'Something urgent has just come up. I'll write at greater length tomorrow.

'Love and kisses from me and, of course, Linette.'

There was no need for anyone in Poitiers to know exactly the nature of his work. He himself had been somewhat vague about it at the beginning. It was Emile Vannier who had found this job for him. Vannier lived in Paris. He was in business, and had the air of a man of influence. One day, when he was in Poitiers visiting his brother, who was a lawyer, Gérard, who was acquainted with him, happened to run into him in a café just at the time when he was desperately anxious to get away from home at all costs.

'I would so much appreciate a word with you, Monsieur Vannier. You know how things are with my family. My father is dead. I am in duty bound to help support my mother, and I'm shortly getting married. Would it be possible for you, with your business connections, to find some opening for me in Paris?'

It was late at night. He had been to a movie. The café was almost empty. They were drinking halves of beer. The waiters were beginning to stack the folding tables.

'Look, I'd better be frank with you. I know you won't betray my confidence. . . .'

And he had told him. The whole truth. Linette was pregnant. He loved her. He wanted to do the right thing by her. But it was absolutely vital for them to get away. The words had poured out in a feverish torrent.

'Above all, if you should meet her, please don't let on that you know. You do understand, don't you?'

Well, it had worked! A few days later, he received a note:

'I had a word with my old friend, Jean Sabin. He has a vacancy for a young man in the clerical department of his organization. Write and tell him how soon you will be free to join his staff.'

And that was how word had got about in Poitiers that he had been offered the job of private secretary to the novelist. They would believe almost anything in Poitiers! They were out-and-out provincials, knowing nothing of the outside world. How, for instance, could they possibly imagine that a famous novelist would be living on the ground floor of that crumbling mansion at the end of a passage leading to the Rue Daru? It was the Headquarters of the League of Patriotic Frenchmen, and he was the President. The place was both his office and his home.

Gérard, in common with Mademoiselle Berthe and Monsieur Drouin, was, in actual fact, an employee of the League. And Auvinet, though he had now been on the staff for a whole month, had never exchanged so much as a word with the novelist.

'Shall I come back here when I've finished?'

Drouin glanced at his watch.

'I shouldn't bother.'

Having stuffed the forty-five envelopes addressed to the newspapers into his pockets, Gérard sprinted down the stairs and got into the taxi, which still retained faint traces of the scent used by the previous occupant.

'Same as usual?'

'Yes. First stop *L'Echo de Paris*.'

In the Faubourg Saint-Honoré, he was tempted to knock on the dividing window. On two previous occasions, when he was doing the rounds of the newspaper offices, he had taken the opportunity to stop at their hotel in the Rue de l'Etoile, to invite Linette to join him. On the last occasion he had found her fast asleep, fully dressed on the bed, for, truth to tell, she had nothing to occupy her, day after day, from morning till night.

'I haven't time today,' he told himself.

And yet this was not altogether true, and he knew it. He was happier on his own, huddled in the corner in the back of the taxi, gazing out absently at the passing lights. From time to time, the taxi would plunge into the thick of the traffic. When they stopped at crossroads, he would watch the limousines draw up outside some imposing mansion, and sometimes glimpse a society beauty in the tastefully

23

upholstered interior, or the smartly uniformed chauffeur of some important personage, wearing an expression of haughty indifference.

It was a cool, damp evening. They were approaching the Grands Boulevards. Auvinet felt the now familiar twinge of feverish excitement, which brought colour to his cheeks.

Anything was preferable to the never-ending flood of envelopes over which he often crouched for days on end. Was he really serving any useful purpose at the League? More often than not, they seemed at a loss to find something for him to do. They sent him on errands, delivering letters, despatching telegrams, or even to sign a memorial book at some funeral parlour on behalf of Jean Sabin, whose signature he too had learned to forge. And on his return, Drouin, who had scarcely more to do than he had, would say, 'You'd better do some envelopes.'

These envelopes were addressed to the League's several thousand members. Thus when it was a question of sending out circulars, the work was half-completed in advance. He had already addressed seven or eight batches of these hateful envelopes, made of coarse, greyish paper, on which it was difficult to get the ink to flow.

Watch out! The Place de l'Opéra. The taxi was jammed in a four-lane crush of traffic, and all the drivers were hooting at the same time. He had learned the trick of leaping out of the cab, and weaving his way through a maze of wheels and radiators, thus gaining a few seconds, reaching the other side of the square, and taking the stairs at a run in the building that housed *L'Echo de Paris*.

Every minute gained was money in his pocket. Drouin had told him, 'The grand tour ought to clock up about forty-five francs on the meter.'

But by speeding things up a little, he could make three or four francs for himself, sometimes more. Even if there had been nothing in it for him, it would have made no difference, because there was something a little intoxicating about this frantic dash through the milling throng of Paris. He was going somewhere. He had a job to do. He was the representative of the League. He was the representative of Jean Sabin.

The receptionist, seated at his desk in the middle of the lobby, knew who he was. Nevertheless, he always announced himself, 'Jean Sabin's secretary. For Monsieur Potut.'

And he went boldly into a large, softly-lit, rather old-fashioned room, furnished with fine rugs, tapestries and antiques, where old gentlemen in pale grey spats and with dangling monocles sat waiting in armchairs. Often they were kept waiting for a long time, while he, Auvinet, who had arrived from the provinces barely a month before, strode confidently up to a door which no one else dared to approach, rapped sharply, and went in without waiting for an invitation.

'From Jean Sabin. Urgent.'

He had learned from Drouin, who had once accompanied him on the grand tour to show him the ropes, that the name must be pronounced resonantly and confidently, even emphatically! Sounding just like Jean Sabin himself, in fact!

'It's for the next edition, is that clear?'

He was on his way again, dashing round the corner of one of the boulevards, entering another building, climbing more stairs. These were the offices of *Le Gaulois*. Another handsome room, a group of elegant women conferring in undertones, a long corridor smelling of printer's ink, a little old man with dandruff, who nevertheless was a well-known public figure, and who dropped the envelope on top of a stack of others on his desk.

Désiré, waiting for him at the door, guided him to the taxi, which was parked a little way off.

'Rue de Richelieu . . . *Le Journal*. . . .'

The pace quickened. And the feverish excitement. Gérard kept an anxious eye on the white-faced clocks here and there. In the offices of *Le Journal* there were endless corridors and staircases to be taken at a run.

L'Evénement . . . La Gazette de la Bourse. . . . Men of affairs, very much on their dignity, were everywhere, receptionists wearing frigid expressions, keeping all comers waiting, endlessly waiting, with the rare exception of some privileged person, who sailed past with a condescending wave of the hand.

One day he too would sail past like that, gaining admission to the inner sanctums. He knew it, he was sure of it, he was determined. And Désiré was there, as usual, waiting for him.

'Faubourg Montmartre'.

La Victoire . . . L'Appel. . . . Then a long diversion through the back streets, cluttered with delivery vans, to reach the sumptuous offices of *Le Petit Parisien* in the Rue d'Enghien.

'From Jean Sabin . . . for the next edition.'

And yet, as he very well knew, all this frenetic activity was to no significant purpose. These innumerable pieces of paper, signed with a flourish by Mademoiselle Lange, who could so skilfully forge her employer's pretentious handwriting, were so banal that they would occupy no more than a paragraph of very small print on the fourth page.

'From Jean Sabin.'

Le Matin. . . . It was time now to turn back towards Saint-Augustin. He had a little time in hand. The meter was showing only thirty-seven francs.

'That will be all, Désiré.'

'What about the other calls?'

He had not the courage to tell him that he would complete the round on foot.

'It's not the grand tour tonight.'

And he hurried along the pavements, bumping into people, brushing against the brilliantly lighted shop-windows. By the end, his legs were a little unsteady, his body damp with sweat, his breath scorching his throat, and yet he wished it could go on for ever.

The last of the envelopes had been delivered. He was back once more in the Place de l'Opéra. It was six o'clock. Mademoiselle Berthe, serene, smiling, conscientious as ever, was putting the cover back on her typewriter, stacking her shorthand notebooks in a neat pile, putting away her carbons and pencils. Finally, she removed the pink cardigan she always wore in the office, and went to put on her hat in front of the mirror.

This was also the moment when the Major popped his head round the door on his way out, to see if Drouin was ready to join him for their regular evening drink of *mandarin-grenadine* in a bar in the Place des Ternes. Only Mademoiselle Lange stayed on. One could never tell what time she would be ready to leave, as she always stayed on in case her services were needed by His Lordship. And sometimes the Great White Chief would forget all about her, and, without a word to her, would go out to dinner in town, leaving her stranded until nine or ten at night, even though she lived out in the suburbs with her mother.

Gérard decided that he too would treat himself to a drink, telling himself that he had to make a phone call anyway.

'Hello! Hôtel de l'Etoile? Listen, madame. I would be much obliged if you would do me the great favour of calling Madame Auvinet to the telephone. Only if she is available, naturally . . . I do beg your pardon . . . yes, it's her husband . . . yes, it is urgent.'

He could hear a shrill voice calling, 'Gaston! Go and see if number 26 is in. . . .'

It was a very small hotel, more of a rooming-house, really. An imitation marble plaque was inscribed: 'Rooms to let by the day or month. All mod. cons. Running hot and cold water.'

The entrance lobby was light, the lift white and the carpet red. But the proprietor and his wife treated the Auvinets

27

with scarcely concealed hostility. They were not their sort of people. There had been one altercation already, when Linette had used the handbasin to wash a few small items of clothing.

'Haven't you read the notice on the door? Cooking and laundry are forbidden in the bedrooms.'

Regardless of this, they had bought a spirit stove because they could not afford two meals a day in a restaurant. At first they had bought ready-cooked food from a dairy in the Avenue des Ternes. Because of the smell, they had had to heat things up on the window sill. Even so, they were found out, because of the smell of stale food that always clung about the room. The rooms on the first and second floors were rented exclusively by the hour, and often they were occupied for no more than a few minutes. Women were always coming in and out. They were on friendly terms with the landlady.

'Don't bother to show me up, Madame Bertrand. I'll take number 6.'

Lurking furtively behind, there was always a man.

'Hello! Is that you?'

Every time he heard his wife's voice on the telephone, it came as a slight shock. She always sounded odd, somehow, and it made him feel a little uneasy.

'Has she been snooping again. . . ? Were you in bed. . . ? No. . . ? What have you been doing. . . ?

'Nothing.'

'Right . . . listen . . . I'm in the Place de l'Opéra . . . on the corner . . . come and meet me . . . we'll have a bite to eat at the Dîners Parisiens . . . what's that . . .? Leave that to me . . . you needn't worry, I can afford it. . . .'

He had made six francs profit on the taxi. The price of the dinner was five francs a head. So . . .

'Hurry up, pet . . . I'll be waiting for you at the bus stop. . . .'

Dutifully, he blew her a kiss. Then, having a little time to kill, and to keep his spirits up, he treated himself to another aperitif, though not without some slight misgivings.

One had to face facts, however. Tomorrow, at all costs, he would have to approach the Major. There was no earthly reason why he shouldn't be paid a month's salary in advance. Surely it made sense? Why should he have to wait thirty days to be paid for his labour? Why should he be under any obligation to lend money to his employers? For that, in a sense, was what the present arrangement entailed.

He was not looking forward to it. The Major was always very civil to him. He was civil to everyone. All the same, there was no disregarding that chilly glint in his pale eyes.

'I'll go and see him in his office. Or maybe I could join them for a drink after work, and then, quite casually on our way out of the bar, I'll say . . .'

Even so, it would still leave him short. He owed a week's rent for the room. And, what was much more distressing, he had already helped himself to five hundred francs from the petty cash.

As for his mother, he had not yet sent her a penny. Nor had he paid a single instalment towards the money outstanding on his dinner jacket. He had already sold it to a pawnbroker in the Rue des Blancs-Manteaux for only two hundred francs. Linette, who had been with him, had protested that it was daylight robbery. She had tugged at his arm to try and get him out of the shop, but, in spite of this, he had accepted the offer.

It was all so unfair. He was only twenty. He was full of good intentions. But no one believed in him. His mother, for instance, had never shown him anything but mistrust.

When his father had died, leaving them more or less destitute, he had made up his mind on the spot to leave school, feeling almost light-hearted about it – well, no, that was not really the case, even though his work had been below standard that year, and his prospects of moving up had been poor.

'You must see, Gérard, that, placed as we are, your best course would be to learn a trade.'

He had done so. From one day to the next, he had renounced all his ambitions. He had given up cleaning his nails. He had grown careless of his appearance. He had applied for a job with a printer, who was a family friend. He had endured humiliation upon humiliation. He had been made to run errands. He had even been allotted the chore of sweeping the workshop!

Was it his fault that he had fallen foul of his employer, who had cancer of the stomach, and a filthy temper?

'Don't you see, Mother, that the best thing for me at my age is to do my military service, and get it over? If I volunteer before I'm called up, I'll be younger than most when I'm released, and there'll be plenty of time then to decide on a career.'

He had had the best intentions. Why, then, had his mother replied, in a doleful voice, like some kind of martyr,

'Only good-for-nothings enlist in the army.'

He had enlisted, nevertheless. He never changed his mind, once it was made up. But before taking the final step, he had returned to the charge. He had put his case eloquently. Sometimes, he even wept. Only as a last resort had he presented his mother with a *fait accompli*.

'Can't you understand how heartbreaking it is for someone of my age to be thwarted at every turn, to be pressured into renouncing everything?'

Money! That's what it always came down to. And never being free of a sense of appalling mediocrity! From the Training Centre he had written:

'Tonight, as always, I am alone in barracks. All my mates have gone into town for the evening, but I have no money left, so I can't even go to the canteen. It's not that I'm lacking in guts! I know life isn't a bed of roses for you either, but . . .'

Money! Money! Money! It stabbed him to the heart, so that he wanted to scream.

30

There was no point in brooding on it. The two aperitifs were doing their work, making him feel warmer and a little more cheerful. He was waiting for Linette to arrive on the bus. There she was, looking at him in some surprise.

'Have you got any money?'

Linette too!

'Look! I've managed to wangle a little extra money. It's only a few francs, but it's been so long since we last went out to dinner.'

'Only the day before yesterday. . . .'

'That was different. It was my birthday.'

And he guided her towards the Impasse Jouffroy, which was bathed in soothing, golden light. Together, they climbed an oak staircase leading to a huge dining-room, enriched with lustrous gilding, where hundreds of people were seated at tables.

If it was not exactly luxury, perhaps, it was a fair imitation. It was warm with the warmth of human company. The colour scheme was dark red. Waitresses scurried to and fro, laden with plates and dishes. He was already studying the long mimeographed menu, which by now he knew by heart.

'What do you say to *rillettes*, to start with?'

They were served as individual portions in coarse little stoneware pots, a meagre spoonful in each.

'Two *rillettes*, two! And to follow?'

The diners, elbow to elbow, scooped up forkfuls of food at speed. The dishes were slapped down in front of one from behind. You could feel the waitresses' stomachs brushing against you.

Bread was served in abundance, in heaped, gilded baskets, and there was a small flask of wine for each customer. Linette did not drink wine.

'May I?'

One could see oneself in the mirrors, looking animated, with shining eyes. One didn't know one's neighbours. No

31

one knew anyone else. Most of the diners were alone, with only their appetites and their dreams for company.

'Would you like a chocolate éclair?'

'I think I'd rather have some cream cheese.'

And all the while, an unending and tireless stream of waitresses came and went. One paid at the entrance, and received a slip in return.

'One chocolate éclair and one portion of *Gervais* cheese.'

'How did you spend the afternoon?'

'Sewing. When you telephoned, I was just about to go out and buy some cheese.'

She was pale under the rouge she had daubed on her cheeks. And suddenly he felt sorry for her, he was moved, he reached for her hand across the table.

'You weren't too uncomfortable?'

'No. I'm getting used to it.'

'Did you have to wait long for the bus?'

He loved her. He must do. If he had not loved her, he would not have got her pregnant. And besides, when she had told him the news, he had not hesitated. He had said, 'There's nothing to worry about. We'll manage somehow.'

There was no point in worrying over practical details, especially money. In a few months' time, when the child was born, in June probably, they would have it fostered. Then no one need know a thing about it. And later, when it was time for the birth to be officially announced, there could be no recriminations.

'You ought to have taken advantage of the dry weather to get a breath of air. You know what the doctor said.'

She never complained. One could not accuse her of that. But she was apathetic. She acquiesced. That was all. He felt that they were not on the same wavelength.

'Listen, darling. . . .'

They had finished their meal. They would soon have to leave. There was a queue of people at the door, waiting for their table.

32

'Tomorrow I'll talk to the Major. I know he'll understand. And besides, in any event, I must find some way, and
I shall. . . .'

She said, in a tone of voice that reminded him of his
mother, 'You mean you don't want to go straight back to
the hotel?'

She was cutting the ground from under his feet. He had a
horror of being 'understood', especially in a trivial matter
such as this.

Why not fall in with his wishes without comment? She
would anyway. Why force him into putting on an act? It
was humiliating.

'Come on . . . there are people waiting for our table.'

And out in the street he squeezed her arm with more
warmth than usual. The boulevards were deserted. Everyone was at dinner. Behind the net curtains of the smart
restaurants they could see the dance bands.

'You see, pet, there are times when I feel the need of
something to stir me up. You can't imagine what this job of
mine does to me. Because, to put it bluntly, all I am at the
moment is a sort of office boy. Well, you know what
Vannier said to me: "To get on in Paris, the one essential is
never to lose heart".'

She did not respond in any way. They walked on.

'Don't you understand my feelings? Later on, when I've
reached my goal, I'll tell you all I've had to endure.'

He was leading her, seemingly at random, towards the
Gare Saint-Lazare.

'You're not feeling too tired, are you? Would you like us
to take a bus? To go to bed at nine o'clock in that hateful
room, because there's nothing else we can do! Or to join the
bustling crowds in the Avenue de Wagram, and to feel the
heart of Paris beating a hundred yards away. . . .'

'You mean you want to go to the Moulin Rouge?'

They had already been there four times.

'There or some other place. It doesn't matter.'

33

This was not true. It was there he wanted to go, not somewhere else. Precisely why, he couldn't say.

'At this hour there's no entrance fee.'

'Promise me we won't stay out too late.'

'Just as long as it takes to have a cup of coffee.'

'How much money have you got left?'

He had not told her that he had already spent what he had taken from the petty cash. Once a week, the Major gave him two hundred francs to cover the cost of stamps, registered letters, buses and taxis. He recorded his expenses in a little black notebook. By tinkering a bit with the figures, he managed to keep a little for himself, just two or three francs a day. But on Saturday, in two days' time, he would have to account for his expenditure.

'Don't worry. The price of a cup of coffee won't break us,' he sneered.

Why was it, yes, why, that she who loved him never failed to clip his wings whenever he felt the urge to soar a little? He could always find something to sell in the Rue des Blancs-Manteaux. He wasn't yet quite sure what. His overcoat for a start, perhaps, seeing that the weather was now warm enough for him to make do with a raincoat.

'Come on.'

The foyer, already cheerful with gusts of warm air and the strains of music. The box office on the right, mercifully still showing the sign: 'Admission free'. In ten minutes or a quarter of an hour it would cost two francs a head to get in, and later in the evening, five. There were still plenty of vacant tables surrounding the dance floor in the vast auditorium, with an orchestra at each end, and at the back the boxes which, later on, would fill up with people in evening dress, drinking champagne.

The strains of a tango filled the auditorium, and the dance floor was bathed in violet light. The crowd was made up of much the same kind of people as at the Dîners Parisiens, clerks, typists, shop assistants, or the unemployed hoping for better things in the future. Both places were worlds of illusion, the one selling the illusion of abundant food and luxury, the other, of glamour and dreams fulfilled.

And the pale faces on the dance floor wore the same grave, far-away expressions as the diners in the restaurant, scooping up their *rillettes* from their little pots, or digging their forks into the pale creamy filling of their éclairs.

'Are you all right?'

'Yes.'

After a slight hesitation he regretfully ordered two coffees from a waiter; he would so much have preferred to have ordered two liqueurs. He didn't care what kind. Bénédictine, Cointreau, Vieille, Cure, magically evocative names, bottled dreams, standing in rows behind the huge bar, staffed with awe-inspiring barmen.

'You see, my dear . . .'

What? What was it he wanted to say to her? He could not find the words. He grasped the tips of her fingers and squeezed them, with loving emphasis.

'I'm so sure. . . .'

His other hand closed itself into a fist, a hard, menacing fist, even as he followed the dancers, swaying in time to the music, with his eyes.

It was not conceivable! It would be unjust, odious, hideously undeserved, if, in spite of this seething ferment inside him, he were forced to continue as Jean Sabin's pseudo-secretary, Jean Sabin, who himself . . .

For now at last he could see things as they really were. The famous novelist supported himself at the expense of the League. Everything else was humbug. It was in the name of the League, composed of a few thousand imbeciles, that he deepened and projected his voice, to the point where the telephone receiver vibrated. The name of the League opened the doors of every newspaper office, and the League paid the rent of the ground floor of the building in the Impasse Daru, where he slept on a divan in his office.

'You couldn't possibly understand, darling, but all those people out there . . .'

Both his fists were now tightly clenched, and it was impossible to tell towards whom his furious aggression was directed: at those poor, foolish couples' swaying on the dance floor to the sounds of the orchestra, and who would shortly be returning to their tables, docile and absorbed, with a cup of coffee in front of them, or the others, still mere shadows in his mind, those gentlemen in pale grey spats, with the rosette of the Legion of Honour in their button-holes, who crowded the elegant waiting rooms of *Le Figaro* or *Le Gaulois,* or the busy personages who jostled the doormen of *Le Journal* or *Le Matin.* . . .

Or maybe it was just that woman dancing over there, wearing sheer black silk stockings and a revealing black silk dress, her mouth thick with lipstick, red as blood.

'You'll see, my dear . . . I shall. . . .'

And it would have taken so very little to cause him to burst into tears!

III

Seated at their little table, with its plush cloth of indeterminate colour, on which it always sickened him to set out their food, he watched her standing in front of the mirror, pulling her dress over her head. It blinded her for an instant, then she could see her reflection once more, her expression strained through effort, and her glazed eyes narrowed to slits.

'Would you have preferred to go out?'

'No, of course not!'

They had eaten a little galantine and some bread, nothing else. On the table in front of him was a bit of greasy paper, an empty litre bottle of wine, and two tooth-mugs stained purplish red at the bottom. As in all inferior hotels, the light bulbs were absurdly dim, which made the air seem cloudy with dust.

'Are you still hungry?'

'No.'

'I thought that, as we'd had a good lunch today with your friend Vannier, you wouldn't mind if we . . .'

'You were quite right.'

Every word she said increased his irritation. But it was not her fault. Her silences did nothing to improve matters. In fact, at times, as he paced up and down the room, hemmed in by a wall of silence, he would fly into a rage.

For the moment, he was relatively calm. He remained seated, his pursed lips expressive of increasing bitterness.

'Did you have a drink on your way home?'

'No.'

She was doing her hair. She had lovely hair. He observed the pallor of her neck and shoulders, and the little black tufts under her arms.

He had arrived home at six o'clock to find her in bed. When he got up in the morning to go to work, she scarcely stirred, and he would leave her lying warm and damp between the sheets, where she would often remain until he returned at midday.

In the early days, when he was out running errands for Jean Sabin or the League, he would call back at the hotel and take her with him. Now he no longer did so, for he never found her dressed to go out, and indeed most of the time she wore nothing but a shapeless dressing-gown, which hung on her in drooping folds, like a shabby flag.

'Are you bored?'

'No.'

He knew that they were working up to a scene. He could still have avoided it, but to do so would have meant changing his plans, and he simply couldn't face that.

There were times when the thought of spending the whole evening in this squalid room made him feel exactly like an insect shut up in a cardboard box. And, to make matters worse, out there, within a stone's throw, was the Avenue de Wagram, with its animated crowds, its lights, its dance halls, cinemas and nightclubs; so much to choose from that people could be seen wandering indecisively from one entrance to another. Thinking of all this, he could even find it in his heart to envy those people who spent the evening in that strange, long arcade, with an ebonite horn in one ear, listening to gramophone records.

'Why not put in a little time on your English?'

He responded with an ironic smirk. True, he had bought himself some English textbooks. He had already learned a little at school. He had thought that, as he had every evening free, it would be a good idea to improve his knowledge of the language.

'Are you feeling tired?'

'No, of course not! Why on earth should I feel tired, when I've spent the whole day doing nothing?'

He was standing up now, thin, irritable, with his long hair flung back. He began pacing the room from wall to wall.

'All the same, Gérard, we can't afford to go out every night.'

'You don't say!'

Sitting on the edge of the bed, she peeled off her stockings, and then slipping between the sheets, she stretched out and relaxed. It seemed to him that in this room they were surrounded by a zone of silence, a kind of limbo in which the tiniest sound was monstrously amplified, whereas outside, heard as an indistinct, muted rumble, was life itself. And here he was, threshing about helplessly, anguished, struggling for breath, like a stranded fish.

'Aren't you coming to bed? You haven't told me yet what Vannier had to say.'

'Yes. Well . . .'

He smirked. What had Vannier talked about? They had both visited him at his flat in an attractive, quiet street in the 17th *Arrondissement*, near the Avenue de Villiers. There was a broad staircase and a lift. The brass bells on the waxed oak doorframes were kept highly polished. A little maid in an embroidered apron, of the kind worn in drawing-room comedies, had opened the door to them. The flat was cosy and sweet-smelling. Vannier, dressed up to the nines, just back from the barber's, had introduced them to an attractive woman in a silk dress.

'My wife.'

The table was laid with a snow-white cloth, flowers, glass and silver. Vermouth was served in cut-glass goblets.

'There's just one more guest to come, a close friend, Lefrançois, a businessman with a wide range of important connections. Let's go into my study for a few minutes, and give the ladies time to get acquainted.'

And there: 'Come in, my dear boy. Take a seat. Cigarette?'

He was a man of about forty, with smooth skin and a fresh complexion, his plumpish face dusted with a touch of powder. He came from a good family in Poitiers. His brother, a lawyer, was very highly regarded. It was said of him that he was a bit of a showman, that he made a great song and dance about his business interests in Paris, but that no one had ever got to the bottom of what these really were. Some people even went so far as to say that they had seen him selling soft drinks at the races.

'You won't take it amiss, will you, if I give you a little fatherly advice? Well then, my dear boy, here's one small tip to start with. Here in town, when one is invited to a meal in a private house as opposed to a restaurant, one should never come empty-handed. A bunch of flowers, a cake. . . .'

And as Gérard, crimson with embarrassment, opened his mouth to speak, 'I know . . . You haven't the money . . . That doesn't matter in the least. There are always ways and means. You must understand that, if you want to make your way in the world, there are higher priorities than making ends meet. Here with us, of course, it's of no consequence, but among strangers it would start you off on the wrong foot.'

How would Linette take that? And that was by no means all Vannier had said. He had talked a great deal, interrupting Gérard every time he opened his mouth.

'I know all about it. I started off just like you. I arrived in Paris without a sou . . . and now, look at these.'

He opened a drawer and pulled out handfuls of yellow and green bills, all of them final demands and writs from decorators and upholsterers.

'Do you think I'm ashamed of all this? Quite the opposite, I assure you. It's just another fact of life that doesn't apply in Poitiers. But you'd better get this into your head: here in Paris, the deeper one is in debt, the higher one's standing and the longer one's credit. Credit, that's the magic word. On the other hand, the one unforgivable sin is to be seen to be poor. Well, sonny boy, let's be frank – and don't take this amiss – it's plain for all to see that you're worse than poor, you're destitute. . . .'

He listened to his own voice, watching the smoke from his gold-tipped Egyptian cigarette, the aroma of which permeated the study, and refilled the glasses they had brought with them with golden vermouth.

'You're still too much of a newcomer to Paris to understand. But you will in time. For instance, there's no shame in unloading crates of vegetables at night in Les Halles. At a pinch, you could even get away with sleeping under the bridges, or selling newspapers in the street. I know someone who started life by selling newspapers, and who is now the manager of three large theatres. But what makes a really bad impression is that pinched look of yours, the look of a docile little underling. . . . I hope I don't sound too discouraging?'

'No.'

'I'll give you the address of my tailor. As soon as you have a little money to spare . . . I wish I could help you there, but the way things are at the moment. . . . But you'll manage, one way or another. There's always plenty of money about, always bear that in mind. You have to learn how to get your hands on it, that's all. Above all, you can't go begging, cap in hand. A good tailor, a good shoemaker, and your head held high . . . . Come on, I think I hear the bell. That will be my friend Lefrançois. We're on to something big at the moment, that ought to net the two of us as much as four or five million francs. A deep-water harbour being built in North Africa, with the help of a government subsidy.'

As they were leaving the study, he stopped.

41

'Just one more word of advice. Don't be seen about too often with your wife just at present. You did the decent thing, I realize that. That's your affair. But it's just not done for a woman in her condition to parade herself in public. It's an embarrassment all round. Considering your age, people will begin wondering whether you're going to go on producing children, like a rabbit. . . .'

Lefrançois had brought a cream cake from one of the best confectioners in town. He was even better dressed, more scrubbed, more scented than Emile Vannier. He had kissed Madame Vannier's hand, then Linette's, somewhat to her surprise. The two men had talked business, dropping names unknown to Gérard. At half past one he had had to leave, in order to get back to the League on time. After the three different wines that had been served with the meal, his head was swimming.

'You'd like to go out, wouldn't you? You might as well own up, you're just dying to go out.'

Furiously he snapped, 'No!'

And he looked at her almost with hatred. There were times when she behaved towards him just like his mother. She could read his thoughts. He had an absolute horror of this, and of her uncomplaining way of saying, '*You might as well admit . . .*'

'You're being unreasonable, Gérard. We've been out almost every day this week. Only last night we went to Montmartre.'

'So what?'

'You were the one who suggested that you might find it useful to study English in more depth. And not once, since you bought all those books, have you. . . .'

He bent his head, looking like a sullen schoolboy avoiding the stern eye of a scolding master.

'How can you think of going out, if you . . .?'

'Go on!'

'You know very well what I'm trying to say.'

'Never mind that. Just say it!'

'We're spending money we haven't got. We have nothing but debts. I'm scared of going into the local shops, because I owe money everywhere.'

'Am I to blame for that?'

'Am I? How much have you got in your pocket?'

'I have no idea . . . . If you really want to know. . . .'

And, taking her by surprise, he drew a fistful of coins from his pocket, threw them on the bed, and took a few notes of small value from his wallet.

'Count it . . . yes, I mean it. Go on! Count it! And then see where it gets us!'

She buried herself deeper under the bedclothes, until all he could see of her was one eye glaring at him from the pillow.

'You see, my dear, there's one thing you always seem to forget, and that's that I'm only twenty.'

His voice hoarsened. He began pacing up and down more rapidly. Then, coming to a sudden halt near the door, he started banging the wall violently with his fists. The pain brought tears to his eyes.

'Don't you see, I'm miserably unhappy, I no longer know where to turn. I . . . I . . .'

'Come here!'

He shook his head.

'Come here, you poor big baby. Don't make me get out of bed. You know I haven't been feeling at all well these past few days. Sit down over here. . . .'

In the end he did as she asked, staring gloomily at the floor.

'I know how painful it is for you, with things the way they are. I realize that you've taken on a heavy burden of responsibility. . . .'

No! No and No! He felt his stomach heave and his gorge rise. His eyes prickled. She didn't understand. She would

43

never understand. No one understood him, and he was seized with a sudden loathing of Vannier, who understood him least of all.

There he was, miserably unhappy, trapped in this hateful room, grazing his knuckles against the walls. He heard other couples coming upstairs, he heard a door shutting. He ground his teeth and clenched his fists.

What was the use of attempting this or that, of trying to learn English, for God's sake? There was no way out, he was done for!

And he repeated aloud, 'I'm done for!'

As for that other fellow, the conceited idiot! How dare he reproach him for not bringing flowers, and advise him to go to a good tailor, when he himself hadn't a sou to bless himself with, let alone lend to a friend in need!

'Done for, do you understand? You're right, we owe money all over the place, and it wouldn't surprise me if, one of these days, the League were to throw me out on my ear. And then what? Eh? Oh! I'm not blaming you for anything. It's entirely my fault. I'm the one who's a fool. What qualifications have I? What am I good for? Tell me that.'

The crisis had reached its peak, exhausting itself in the process, and he ended up by flinging himself face down on the bed, sobbing hoarsely and quivering from head to foot.

She dared not so much as move a muscle, but lay watching him in silence, as he repeated, 'Done for . . . that's the real truth. All the rest is crap. When I think . . . when I think. . . .'

All his dreams! For he had dreamed with all his heart and soul, such dreams. . . .

'Calm down, Gérard. Even supposing we can't make it in Paris, we can always try our luck in Gabon, like my sister and her husband.'

Why suggest that, of all things? Was she incapable of the smallest glimmer of understanding? He could hear another

44

voice, that of his mother, so sharpened with malice that he could still feel the wound.

'Can't you see what these people want to drive you to? Well, then, I'll tell you. They have a daughter living in Gabon. According to them, she's managing to put aside a thousand francs a month out there. Well, what they want is to see you shunted off there, too! Your wife would like nothing better, I'm sure, because out there they have house-boys, so she wouldn't have to do any cooking or housework. She could just spend the day stretched out on her bed, giving orders. No matter if you should finish up like most of the others, crippled by some tropical disease, or drinking your-self to death!'

And another thing she had said, this mother of his, 'Can't you see they were out to get you? They foisted her on you, leaving them sitting pretty, with only one more daughter out of three to marry off. And you mark my words, it won't be long before they find some other young idiot for that one.'

And now he found himself wondering whether there wasn't, perhaps, a grain of truth in what she had said. It was as if the woman lying beside him, his wife, were suddenly a stranger.

He was appalled at the thought, for if she too was lost to him, there would be nothing left.

'Why are you looking at me like that? What have I done to upset you?'

He was wondering. It was absurd, really, but he couldn't shake off the notion that he had perhaps been caught in a trap. His mother didn't know the whole story. If she had, she would, he felt sure, have gone even further.

'I wouldn't be surprised if she did it deliberately.'

To get herself pregnant! To entrap him into marriage!

He was working himself up again, banging the walls again, sobbing, grinding his teeth. But when the fever had subsided a little, he was able to catch a fleeting glimpse of what this outburst was really all about.

45

The truth of the matter was that he wanted to go out, that he had made up his mind to go out, and nothing would stop him. The moment had come. Linette was looking at him with compassionate understanding.

'Come here, you great baby!'

And, seeing that he would not move, she got out of bed in her nightdress and threw her arms round him.

'Come on, now! There's no need to look at me like that, as if you hated me. It's all because of the way things are. I know there are times when you lose faith in yourself, but you're wrong, you know you are. You'll succeed in time, you'll see. You've got what it takes . . . . Remember, in Poitiers, how we used to look in through the lighted windows in those streets near the railway station?'

And how they used to cling together, her warm body pressed against his, in some dark corner.

'You used to say . . .'

He was calmer now. His rage and antagonism had subsided, and he now looked merely sulky. Then, at long last, he managed a faint smile. He was still snuffling a little.

'We're here together at any rate, the two of us, just as we'd always hoped. All the rest will follow. It must. Everyone goes through a bad patch at some time. It was I who was at fault just now. I ought to have understood your need to get away, to wander about the streets, among the lights and the people. Do you mind very much my not coming with you? I honestly don't feel up to it.'

He shook his head, and she bent down, gathered up the notes and small change, and slipped them into his pocket.

'Go on, go out. Have a drink somewhere.'

Pride forbade him to yield so easily. He said, with less conviction, perhaps with no conviction at all, 'I'm a failure.'

'You're a great big softie! For one thing, no one can call himself a failure at the age of twenty. It was you who reminded me just now that you are only twenty.'

'Well, I do feel . . .'

46

'Do as I say. Go and get a breath of air.'

After some further show of reluctance, he eventually picked up his hat and raincoat.

'I'll just go as far as the corner. I've got a headache. Sitting for hour upon hour in that office, addressing envelopes . . . that's what my job consists of! Can you imagine what it's like?'

'I think I'll be asleep before you get outside the door. Give me a kiss.'

He kissed her, endeavouring to rekindle the passion he had felt in the windy streets of Poitiers.

'Do you remember, whenever you stopped and kissed me, it always seemed to be right under a gas lamp?'

Before putting on his hat, he combed his hair and splashed water on his face. As he was about to shut the door, she called him back.

'Don't forget. . . .'

And she pointed to the crumbs and greasy paper, scattered all over the table. For they had to be careful not to antagonize the proprietress, to obliterate all traces of the meal they had eaten.

He got rid of the lot in a dustbin in a dimly lit street near the Etoile. With every step he took, he stood taller, and his feet tapped more briskly on the pavement. And there at last were the lights and the crowds of the Avenue de Wagram. Voluptuously he plunged into the throng.

And yet the thrill he felt was not without a tinge of bitterness, which he aggravated, as one aggravates a toothache by probing the cavity with one's tongue. He was all alone in that great crowd. All around were the people of Paris, an immense, unapproachable community, and he threaded his way among them with a feeling of anguish, searching for other lonely people, who like him were there in search of a little human warmth.

That was something Linette would never understand. She knew nothing of these fits of anguish, taking him

47

suddenly by the throat for no apparent reason, to which he had always been subject. Even in Poitiers. For instance, in the days when he had worked at the printers, Dumur. He recalled the rhythmic clatter of the machines, and the procedures followed by the craftsmen all around him, which never varied, almost as though they had remained unchanged since the dawn of time.

Everything there was black and white, dense black and harsh white, and suddenly he would get the feeling that he had lost touch with reality, that all the life had gone out of living. He could see himself, still in front of the mirror, engulfed in stillness. It had seemed as if the world were closing in on him. There was no longer anything but those harsh white walls and those black, intricate machines. Would he ever manage to escape, or would his whole life slip away from him in this way?

Later, when he had gone to work for Monsieur Malterre in that big office, lined from floor to ceiling with green filing cabinets, with its stove in the middle of the grey wood floor, the great flue that ran from end to end of the room, and the staff tapping away on their typewriters, he would again suddenly be a prey, usually just as the lights were being switched on, to this same onset of panic.

At such times, he would be filled with a desperate need to escape at all costs. He was terrified. Surely this could not possibly be all that life had to offer. He had to break out of this mould. He needed to breathe. Without realizing it, having paused for a moment opposite the posters above the door of a cinema, he found himself at the illuminated entrance of the Empire. It was the interval, and some members of the audience had come out into the street for a smoke.

A little while ago, he would have given anything on earth to get away from that nightmarish room, in which his whole life seemed to be tied to the bed and its surroundings.

Maybe he would turn out to be a failure. Suddenly, it seemed almost something to be desired, because a failure, after all, was without roots or obligations, like that old man over there, wandering among the crowds, selling crumpled newspapers.

It almost made him laugh. Here he was with a wife, and a mother who had little or nothing to live on without his support. And what was more, there was a child coming. And yet, in spite of this, with all this great, crushing weight on his shoulders, he was only twenty years of age, and utterly alone.

What was he fit for? Nothing! He didn't even know any English. He had bought the textbooks, but he hadn't read them. He had no qualifications. All he was fit for was to be an office boy. Nothing else! The only alternative was to go and bury himself in Gabon, like his brother-in-law.

He turned the corner into the Avenue des Ternes.

Truth to tell, he had no idea where he was going. This was only the third or fourth time he had been out at night after his wife was in bed, giving as his excuse that he had a headache, or that he had better go down and get rid of the scraps left over from their supper.

There was a bistro in the Avenue des Ternes, with a bar counter, four or five little tables, and a bustling waiter. The lighting was exceptionally bright, almost too much so. Opposite was a much larger, almost luxurious bar, where he was in the habit of having his breakfast of coffee and croissants. It suited him well enough in the morning.

But at night he preferred the smaller place. He liked the harsh glare of the lighting. There was something about the atmosphere that suggested dubious, even murky associations. He couldn't quite put his finger on it. There were several men leaning on the counter, most of them unaccompanied, men who were strangers to him, about whom he knew nothing. He had no idea where they came from or where they were going.

49

'A brandy.'

He joined them at the bar, and stood there looking about him absently. He could have stayed there for hours, God knows why. Occasionally a woman would come in from the street, to have a look.

There was one there tonight, sitting all alone at a table at the back of the café. They had already exchanged glances. She was sitting idly, leaning her elbows on the table, with a glass in front of her. Her coat hung open, revealing a close-fitting black silk dress, which outlined her firm, round breasts.

He was attracted at first glance. Linette had been in a good deal of pain recently. Because of her condition, it was now several weeks since he and she had made love. And besides, he no longer felt the urge. He could never forget the child inside her, and it made him feel uncomfortable.

The brandy scorched his throat. As a sort of gesture of defiance, he ordered another. He went on gazing at the young woman, and she stared back. Eventually, she smiled at him. Was it a mocking smile, a playful response to his fierce scowl? Catching sight of himself in the mirror, he thought it probably was, and flushed.

Then, when he turned from the mirror to look at her again, her smile broadened. She seemed to find the situation highly entertaining. He scowled.

He was in a highly nervous state that evening. He was within an ace of throwing his money down on the counter and stalking out. At the same time he was overwhelmed with a burning desire for her, a fevered excitement such as sometimes follows a storm of tears.

What did she want from him? She kept looking at him, and then, with a radiant smile, at the empty chair facing her. He hesitated, then went up to her. He did not take the chair, but, still standing, said, 'You're making fun of me, aren't you?'

'No, not in the least, I assure you.'

She had a lilting voice, with a marked Spanish accent. She was prettier than any other woman he had ever accosted. Pretty and fragile-looking, like a little statuette.

'Won't you sit down?'

He did so awkwardly, still suspecting that she was making fun of him.

'What were you thinking about?'

'Me? I don't know. Why?'

'You looked so fierce! It was as if you were spoiling for a fight with someone. When you looked at me, I wondered whether you were going to attack me. Don't you like me?'

Still in that lilting voice, revealing small, gleaming teeth as she spoke, and the tip of a sensual pink tongue. Her eyes sparkled like those of a child. The waiter came up to them, and Gérard asked, 'What will you have?'

'Whatever you think . . . something sweet . . . I can see you haven't been long in Paris.'

'Two months. How can you tell?'

'I don't know.'

And he was surprised to discover that there was something like tenderness, as well as mockery, in her voice. He was shabbily dressed. He hadn't needed Vannier to tell him that. His fawn raincoat was crumpled and soiled. He had a large pimple on his forehead.

'What a strange boy you are.'

The time passed very quickly. He talked at random, scarcely knowing what he was saying. He could not take his eyes off her. She was still watching him, her face aglow with good-humoured mockery.

'If you only knew . . .' he murmured, sounding troubled and a little hoarse.

'If only I knew what?'

'How much I long for you.'

She burst out laughing, and then suddenly fell silent. Her expression was grave now, almost as if she were a little afraid of him.

51

'Just like that!' she teased.

'Please don't laugh at me.'

'We've only just met. You don't even know my name.'

'Tell me.'

'Pilar.'

'Is that your surname?'

She laughed again.

'Of course not! It's my Christian name. It's a Spanish name. I'm Spanish.'

'Listen . . . we absolutely must. . . .'

'This very minute, you mean?'

'Yes.'

Then, after a slight hesitation, she began looking about for the waiter, who was serving a customer nearby.

'You'd better pay the bill.'

Before he knew it, he was in the street, and she was at his side.

'You're a strange boy.'

She shivered slightly. As for him, he didn't even know whether he would have to pay her. Walking along beside her, he stammered, 'Where are we going?'

She looked at him again. She was intrigued, yet a little scared.

'Follow me.'

For a moment, he thought she was taking him to the hotel where he lived, but she went past it, stopped a little further on at the door of a respectable-looking building, rang the bell, went inside, and murmured her name to the concierge in passing.

'Don't make a sound,' she whispered.

He found himself inside her flat, a delightful little place, very light and cheerful, and attractively furnished. She was laughing. She asked, not in the least embarrassed by the implications of her question, 'What did you expect?'

Whereupon he literally threw himself at her, grasping her in his arms, half-stifling her.

52

'You might at least give me a chance to take off my coat!'

When he looked at his watch, he saw that it was one o'clock in the morning. He had talked for hours, he had, in a sense, become intoxicated by the torrent of words he had poured out, baring his soul, telling her everything about his past, his fears for the future, his innermost thoughts and feelings, as she lay, cheek to cheek beside him, watching him with those tenderly mocking eyes of hers.

'Come on, now. It's time you went home to your wife.'

'Yes.'

'What are you going to say to her?'

'I don't know . . . I'll think of something.'

'Is this the first time you've been unfaithful to her?'

He nodded.

'To think you didn't know the first thing about making love! Come here.'

And she stood him under the lamp, scrutinized his face and neck, and wiped away all traces of facepowder and lipstick.

'Let me see. No, your hair doesn't smell of scent, but your breath! You'd better have something strong to drink before you go home.'

He could still see her, completely naked, more than ever like a little statuette, watching him from the doorway as he went down the stairs. Then he was out in the street, walking past the bar where they had met. There were only two customers left now, tossing down one last drink.

Stealthily he climbed the hotel stairs, two at a time, without making a sound. Linette opened her eyes.

'Weren't you able to sleep?'

'Is it late? I think I dozed off.'

The room smelt stale. His wife's forehead was damp with perspiration.

'I got talking to someone. Rather an interesting fellow . . . I'll tell you all about it tomorrow.'

And that was the end of that, for the time being.

IV

Just now he had begged her pardon, saying that it was all his fault. But was it really entirely his fault? He had dragged Linette out to the Coliseum, a huge nightclub in the style of the Moulin Rouge, not far from the Boulevard Roche-chouart. As it happened, she had slept all afternoon. He had found her still asleep on his return from the League at six o'clock. Bearing this in mind, he had made a point of remarking, at eleven o'clock, just as the floor show was about to begin:

'I'm so glad you had a good long sleep this afternoon. It means we won't have to worry if we're late getting home.'

That had always been his way, even as a small child: he could never bear to tear himself away from any kind of spectacle or game, however inferior the spectacle, however tedious the game. He was never satisfied unless he was the last to leave, and by the time they had emerged from the Coliseum it was a few minutes past midnight.

There was a Metro station nearby, but also nearby were the boulevards of Montmartre.

'What do you say to a short walk first?' he had suggested. 'Let's at least get a breath of air, before we go to bed.'

His appetite for the sights of Paris was insatiable, the shadowy corners beneath the overhead railway, where couples could be seen sauntering about, the little brightly-lit bistros and brasseries of the Place Pigalle, the steep streets, veiled in mystery, leading up to the Sacré-Coeur

54

and down to the bustling town centre, the neon signs, the cabaret foyers with their doormen in red or blue uniforms.

'I'm sure a walk will do you good. Isn't that what the doctor said?'

He had said nothing of the sort, but no matter. . . .

They could have taken the Metro from the Place Blanche. But that way led only to a dark stretch of deserted boulevard.

'We'll take it from the Place Clichy.'

But, by the time they had got there, the last train had left, and the gates were being closed. There were no buses running by then.

'I'm sorry, Linette, my poor love. You see! If only I'd had my watch. . . .'

He had sold his watch, like so many other things.

'Never mind, we'll take a taxi.'

'No, Gérard, no! We can't afford to waste all that money. And it's not all that far.'

So they had walked. First, the length of the Boulevard Batignolles, then beside the railings of the Parc Monceau, with their gilded finials, and from there to the luxurious mansions of the Boulevard de Courcelles. Every now and then she had shivered.

'Are you feeling cold?'

'No . . . I don't think so. . . .'

'I haven't overtired you, have I?'

Towards the end, even his legs had been aching. When they got to the Avenue de Wagram, there had been one café still open.

'What about a hot toddy, to warm you up before you go to bed?'

'No, Gérard. It would take all we've saved on a taxi.'

He had snapped irritably, 'Whatever you say.'

And the trouble had started as soon as they got to their room. In bed she had shivered with cold. She, who usually lay so still between the sheets, had tossed and turned, and gasped for breath in the dark.

'What's wrong?'

'I don't know . . . It's probably nothing. . . .'

An hour had passed, and she was still wide awake.

'Are you asleep, Gérard?'

'No.'

'I'm so cold.'

He had got up and piled all the clothes he could find on the bed, but by then she was shivering violently, and her teeth were chattering. He had held her close, but to no avail.

'Would you like a hot water bottle?'

Once more he had got out of bed and, in his bare feet, lit the spirit lamp, and filled an empty wine bottle with hot water. It had taken him a little while to find a cork.

'I can't understand it. It's not a bit cold.'

And this was true. For several days now, Paris had enjoyed such warm spring weather that it was being forecast, in the newspapers, that the chestnut tree that always came into flower on the fifteenth of March would bloom early this year.

'I can't breathe, Gérard.'

The hot water bottle, the heaps of clothing, had been no help. Her face had been very flushed, her eyes feverish.

'I'm going to look for a doctor.'

To his amazement, she had agreed. As a rule she would go to any lengths to avoid seeing a doctor. Hastily he had dressed. And from then on it was chaos, a nightmare. The night porter had given him the name of a doctor in the Rue Brey. He had had to ring the bell several times. The doctor had come to the door himself, wearing grubby pyjamas, with his hair all over the place. His bed-sitting room was in a mess, with bottles and dirty glasses everywhere, and a half-dressed woman lying on a divan.

He's a foreigner, A Roumanian probably, thought Gérard.

'I won't be a moment.'

They walked together through the dark streets, deserted

except for an occasional passing car. He had taken Linette's pulse, and looked worried.

'Is it serious, doctor?'

He had subjected her to an exhaustive examination.

'Breathe in. . . . Breathe out. . . . Breathe in. . . . Count 99. . . . No. . . . Say 99. Again, more slowly. . . .'

And now, at a quarter past nine in the morning, Auvinet's head was swimming, his lips burning, and his eyelids drooping.

Years ago, when he was five or six years old, his parents had, over quite a long period, got into the habit of going on an excursion every Sunday. They would set out in the morning, taking a picnic lunch with them. They would walk for miles. His father, who had long legs, always wanted to go a little further.

'You ought to consider the child,' his mother would say.

'When he's tired, I'll carry him.'

They were searching for a pleasant site, a wood or a stream. His father always knew of a better place further on. On the way back, Gérard was always limping. His head seemed too heavy for his shoulders, as if it had swollen in the sun. He could hear the sounds of the countryside only as a confused buzzing in his ears. His father would carry him for a little while, and then put him down. His mother would complain of tiredness.

As for him, by the end of the day he was stupefied, by the light and the heat and the penetrating country smells: sun-baked earth, hay, cows, wild flowers crushed between his fingers.

Returning to the town was like entering another world, an empty, echoing world, very still, in the setting sun, with only a few dark, shadowy figures gliding wearily through the streets. Their house, too, was empty, its special familiar smell now cold and stale, where their dinner had yet to be cooked.

57

He would be put to bed, to fall into an exhausted sleep, troubled with nightmares.

And this morning it was in just such a state of bewildered exhaustion that he ran, bare-headed, towards the offices of the League. At the end of that first visit, in the middle of the night, the doctor had been unable to make a confident diagnosis. He suspected pneumonia, but was not yet quite sure. Gérard had to chase all over the town, losing his way several times, to find a pharmacy that was open.

After that, he had had to heat water time after time, until the fuel for the spirit lamp was all used up. The hotel porter had none to lend him. He paced up and down the room on tiptoe, until, in the end, he collapsed into the only armchair. The only sound was Linette's breathing. It was less rasping now, but she was still tossing and turning restlessly.

Earlier on, soon after the doctor had left, he had burst into tears, begging her forgiveness over and over again.

'Don't! It's not your fault.'

And then she had added, 'Maybe it's all for the best.'

What had she been trying to tell him? That this illness would probably result in a miscarriage? He had raised the question with the doctor.

'I can't make any positive prognosis at this stage.'

Ought she not to be in hospital? It was virtually impossible to look after her properly in this squalid hotel room. And besides, he would not put it past the proprietor to give them notice.

And where was the money to come from? He had already considered sending a telegram: *Linette gravely ill. Come immediately.*

At times like this, all is forgiven. Was there really any other way out?

On the other hand, who could say? Linette might die. No! He did not wish her dead. Of course not! But, all the same, he felt ashamed at having even thought of the possibility, as though it were one among several ways out.

A solution for him, needless to say!

He had done all he could for her. Early next morning the doctor returned, washed and shaven now, with traces of powder behind his ears.

'Don't look so down! It's not as bad as it might have been. It's probably a case of dry pleurisy.'

'Shall I be able to look after her here, doctor?'

'I don't see why not. And besides, the hospitals are so full at the moment, I doubt if they'd take her.'

He had given him detailed instructions about what needed to be done, and what her diet should be. He had written out a long prescription. He had promised to visit her again that evening.

It was a quarter past nine already. Gérard, not knowing whether he was running or walking, turned into the cul-de-sac, went into the offices of the League, and made a dash for the stairs. It was the Major he had to see. He had no time to waste on the ground floor. He bounded upstairs to the first floor, where he hardly ever had occasion to set foot.

To tell the truth, he had been there only once before. On that occasion Drouin had given him something or other, some letters or circulars, to take to the Major. He had knocked on his door. He was sure of that, but he had not waited for a reply. He had flung open the door, and, through a crack in the cupboard door, he had seen the Major hastily shoving a bottle of spirits out of sight.

Only a split second before, Gérard was sure, he had seen him snatch the tilted bottle from his lips. He had made the mistake of murmuring, 'I beg your pardon.'

To begin with, the Major had turned his back on him, presumably to wipe his mouth. And Gérard, feeling very much an intruder, had just stood there. The office, like the one downstairs, had once been a bedroom, with the walls covered in flowered paper, on which the marks of furniture that had formerly stood there could still be seen.

This time, in spite of his sense of urgency, he knocked and waited to be called in. Why, despite this, did he still have the same impression as before, of having taken the Major by surprise? True, he had not been expecting him. At this time of day, as a rule, no one but Mademoiselle Berthe was in the habit of going up to his office.

Through an uncurtained window could be seen the dingy light of the courtyard. The Major was seated at a desk of unstained wood. To his left was a pile of letters, those precious letters that he collected himself from the concierge, and carried like some priceless treasure upstairs to his office.

With a paper-knife he was carefully slitting open the envelopes, most of which contained postal orders or banknotes of various denominations from ten to a hundred francs. These he extracted and stacked, according to their value, in little piles in front of him.

The odd thing was the intensity with which he addressed himself to this task. No, intensity was perhaps not quite the right word. At any rate, he was making no secret of it, since he had shouted, 'Come in!'

It was possibly Gérard's feverish state of mind that made him feel so ill-at-ease. He had been brooding for too long, weeping too much, and had spent the whole night rushing hither and thither. For breakfast, he had just had a glass of spirits, by way of a pick-me-up.

Until now he had looked upon the Major, who was General Secretary of the League, as a man of stature. True, he had held the rank of major only in wartime, but he was still always addressed by his rank. He had seemed a man of culture, always smartly dressed, with the air of one who had perhaps once been a lawyer. It was he who received visits from members of the League, who dictated letters to Mademoiselle Berthe, and who, practically every morning, spent an hour or two closeted with Jean Sabin in his office on the ground floor. He spent hours on the telephone talking to his wife, who was very aristocratic, and to whom he was devoted.

Why, then, did it shock Gérard so much to find him engaged in sorting postal orders and banknotes into little piles? For it certainly did shock him, as if he had involuntarily stumbled upon some act of indecency.

He had no time to dwell on the matter. All the same, it was a revelation he could not ignore. He had finally uncovered the secret of this strange building, tucked away at the end of a cul-de-sac, its rooms turned into offices, its comings and goings, its telephone calls, its notices in the newspapers, and those thousands of envelopes, which he spent day after day addressing and posting, with their enclosed circulars, to the membership.

That great mass of letters, those banknotes of small and large denominations, those postal orders . . . when the Major paid him his salary, or gave him money for his expenses, he always took it from his wallet. He would take the wallet from his pocket, and it was always bulging with notes.

'What's the trouble, young man?'

At this time of day, the Major's eyes were bleary. But Gérard had solved that particular mystery on his previous visit to this floor. The bottle in the cupboard had been explanation enough. In the morning, the Major was always taciturn. He would put his head round the office door, take a quick look, and then immediately retire upstairs to his own domain, with the reddened eyes of a man who had had a sleepless night.

Then, alone in his private retreat, he would wind himself up with the help of his bottle, a little at a time, until he had reached the stage where he was himself again, his tread firm, almost a little too firm, his eyes alert, his expression hard.

There was scarcely a day when he did not have a luncheon engagement in town, from which he always returned very animated and loquacious, his moustache smelling of cigars and liqueurs; and Mademoiselle Berthe had told Gérard, in confidence, that on these occasions, after he had shut himself up in his office, he would take a nap, sitting in his chair, with his head resting on his arms on the desk.

'Please forgive me for disturbing you, Major . . . I'm late, I'm afraid . . . my wife took ill during the night. It's pleurisy. The doctor has already been to see her twice. He was afraid at first that it might be pneumonia.'

'Perhaps you'd better take the day off.'

'No. That won't be necessary, if you don't object to my looking in on her every two hours or so. It's no distance. . . .'

This, however, was not the real purpose of his intrusion. He had spent every centime he had left at the chemist's, and if the doctor were to present his bill, he would be unable to pay it.

'It means a lot of extra expense . . . I'm so confused. . . .'

He truly felt deeply embarrassed, mainly by the sight of all those letters, banknotes and postal orders right under his nose, at which he could not help glancing furtively from time to time.

And then the Major's expression was so inscrutable. He had often wondered what this man really thought of him. He remembered that first interview, when the Major had subjected him to a long and piercing scrutiny.

'And you are all alone in Paris?' he had murmured, as if to himself.

'Except for my wife.'

'And your mother is a widow. . . .'

Why sound so mournful about it? And yet Gérard fancied he could also detect a hint of sympathy, perhaps even compassion, in his tone of voice.

Since that first time, they had scarcely exchanged a word. As a rule, when the Major looked in on the office on the ground floor, he would merely glance at him. At best, when he was in one of his less taciturn moods, he would ask, 'Are you getting used to living in Paris? And your wife?'

On two occasions, Gérard had asked for an advance on his salary. This had gone much more smoothly than he had anticipated. It was as if the Major had been expecting it, and he had merely looked at him with a sigh, then got out his wallet, and counted out the notes.

And now, once again, he was subjecting him to the same bleary-eyed and yet reflective scrutiny.

'What date is it?'

'The ninth.'

Did he want to stress the point that it had not escaped him that Gérard had already run through his salary so early in the month? He took several notes of various denominations from the piles on the desk. He seemed to hesitate, wondering whether to add more. Then he handed them to Gérard.

'You may take as much time off as you need to look after your wife. If necessary, even two or three whole days . . . . But be sure to tell Mademoiselle Berthe.'

It was nothing he could put his finger on, and yet this interview made an impression on Gérard that he could never afterwards shake off. He had never been made to feel so small, so pitiable. Worse than pitiable, of no account.

Worse still, it was not he whom the Major had been looking at, it was not to him that he had given the money. Gérard's eyes were open at last. And as he went down the gloomy staircase, he felt profoundly discouraged.

His predecessor in the job had been a man named Malterne. It was Mademoiselle Berthe who had told him about him. Drouin had been out on an errand, and Mademoiselle Lange had been summoned to Jean Sabin's office. At such times he and Mademoiselle Berthe, alone together, would engage in idle gossip.

For six months, before he took the job, his work had been done by a young man by the name of Malterne, a youth of about his own age, who had been a particular favourite of the

Major's. Gérard gathered that he had been something of a wag, since, whenever his name was mentioned, it was in connection with some witticism or piece of harmless mischief.

'Why did he leave?'

'There was an unfortunate incident.'

Malterne had clearly been guilty of some irregularity. Now Gérard knew what it was. For he had also been told that, in Malterne's time, it had been customary to open the mail in the ground-floor office, and the task of doing so had been entrusted to Malterne.

In his mind's eye, Gérard could see the banknotes and postal orders being slid out of their envelopes.

'Where is he now?'

'He got a job as secretary to a local government official. He's been back here once or twice to see the Major.'

And before Malterne there had been someone else. This had been before Drouin had joined the staff of the League. His name had been Bigois, another young man, twenty-two or twenty-three years old. He had been married, and came from the north – from Lille, was it, or Roubaix? – but he had contracted tuberculosis, and had had to go to the mountains for treatment.

In other words, it was not he, Auvinet personally, upon whom the Major had bestowed that strange, troubled look; it had embraced all the other young newcomers to Paris, all like him, worried, tense, threadbare, and in need of money, always in need of money. Then, in moments of crisis, they would go upstairs, or else they would cheat a little with the petty cash, and, in some cases, even resort to stealing.

He was so exhausted that he opened the wrong door by mistake. Admittedly, he was not in the habit of approaching his own office from the staircase. Still! He opened the door at the rear, and was conscious of a blast of cold, damp air, and an indefinable smell. It was not the first time that he had been in this room either. Like the rest, it was dilapidated. There was even a pane of glass missing from the window – the gap had been filled by an advertising calendar – and the floor was littered with piles of news-papers, posters and circulars.

So this was all the League amounted to! Lying about were all the posters that had adorned the streets of Paris over the last few years, bundles of membership cards, and, in one corner, rolled-up flags and banners.

Downstairs, Jean Sabin, haranguing God knows how many cabinet ministers on the telephone with his inflated rhetoric. Upstairs, the Major, carefully slitting open the envelopes. . . .

'My wife is ill,' he blurted out as he entered his own office.

He told them all about it. He sat down at his desk, and filed some circulars. Then he opened the letter from his mother that he had found in his pigeon-hole on his way out of the hotel. Was this really the best time to read it? As usual, it was plaintive, written in her familiar bitter-sweet style, and, as usual, she expressed herself in the most humiliating terms, leaving him destitute of any hope for the future.

'It's no surprise to me that things have turned out the way they have. I warned you, remember, but you would have none of it, claiming that it was what you wanted more than anything else on earth. Whoever heard of getting married at your age, without a decent job and without prospects?

'As for your mother, when did you ever spare a moment's anxiety for her? Never a word about anyone but yourself, always yourself. Your future to consider . . . as if you were the only one with his way to make in the world.

'I can only hope that your wife may be of some assistance to you, but I doubt it.

'As for me, I shall have to take some positive step soon. But, never you fear, I shall manage somehow. I've had to work all my life, and even at my age I'm still strong and capable.

'I've already put out a few feelers among the neighbours, and I've heard of an old gentleman living alone, who is in need of a servant.'

Servant! She had chosen the word with care. How many times had he heard it from her, spoken out of spite. Yes, spite, because no one knew better than she did that the very suggestion brought tears to his eyes. Even as long ago as when he had volunteered for military service before he was due to be called up, she had threatened him with it!

'Go on, then, if that's what you want. After all, there's nothing I can do to stop you, is there? When you get an idea in your head . . . . As for me, I'll settle for taking a job as a servant.'

Was she incapable of giving him at least a few months' breathing space? All he wanted was enough time to look around. Was that so unreasonable? He could just hear her whining to the neighbours.

'As far as I'm concerned, Madame Bertrand, I might as well have no son. He was determined to get married, and live in Paris. He claims to be earning two thousand francs a month. The best I can say of him is that he hasn't yet gone so far as to ask me for money.'

And far away in the distance, across the courtyards, the sun was beating down on the backs of the big buildings in the Rue de Courcelles. There was one room in particular that he never tired of looking at. It was entirely white, with white-fronted cabinets all the way round, and these cabinets were piled high, in orderly stacks, with leather trunks and suitcases, a sumptuous superfluity of luggage.

Every morning, a valet in a striped waistcoat sat at the open window, brushing suits and coats. Sometimes, he would be joined by a lady's maid, who would stay for a chat. Then one or other of them would leave the room on the trot, no doubt in response to the ringing of a bell.

Drouin would be reading the papers or writing to one of his girl-friends. For there was never an evening when there was not some young woman waiting for him on the corner of the Rue Daru.

His complexion was ruddy, and his skin coarse, but he always looked fresh-faced and well-scrubbed, and he had large, even teeth. It was he who, whenever the League held a parade, was in charge of the organization. Wearing a tricolour armband on his blue suit, he bustled up and down the ranks of participants, giving orders, quickening the pace of the march, seeing that the banners were held at the right angle.

At half past ten he took his watch from his pocket, a gold hunter with a cover opening by means of a spring, of which he was inordinately proud.

'What about taking a few minutes off and looking in on your wife?'

He left the office without his raincoat, for the streets were sunny, and it was a mild spring day. As he went past a dairy, and then a pork butcher's, where cooks were queuing at the counter, he had a lump in his throat, so great was his longing to be able to enjoy the simple pleasures of life like anyone else, to make the most of the hours that were slipping through his fingers.

Suddenly, as he was walking up the Avenue de Wagram, where they were changing the posters outside the cinema, he saw a familiar face, a smile that he recognized, and it troubled him.

It was Pilar, whom he had never seen again since that first time. She was wearing a housedress and no hat, and was carrying several small white parcels. He turned away, intending to avoid her, but he had left it too late.

He had promised to visit her again, but he had not done so. Why not? He would have been hard put to it to explain. Maybe because he was a little afraid of her? Or afraid of himself? Who could tell?

'You're in a great hurry, it seems,' she said, without a trace of ill-humour.

67

Then, looking flustered, he explained, 'My wife is very ill . . . they're not sure yet . . . but it could be pneumonia.'

'Is she in hospital?'

'No, but it may come to that.'

'Poor thing . . . . Has she a temperature? Is that why you haven't been to see me?'

Her expression was even more heart-warming than the spring-like atmosphere of the avenue, with its side-view of the Arc de Triomphe in the distance.

'Have you got someone to look after her?'

'I'm looking after her myself.'

Compassionately, she repeated, 'Poor thing! You poor boy!'

And she tucked a hand under his arm. 'Are you on your way to your hotel?'

'Yes.'

'Wait . . . come with me.'

In a sort of daze, he followed her. He did not think what he was doing. He was engulfed in sunshine and fresh morning scents. She went into a foodshop, and he stood hesitating on the threshold. She beckoned him in.

Very self-possessed, like a strange little fairy godmother, she ran her eye along the marble shelves of the shop, and pointed to this and that with a rosy fingertip.

'Those, yes . . . . Are they very sweet?'

Muscat grapes, big elongated grapes, then some dates, then . . . 'Shut up! It's none of your business! They're for your wife.'

And she repeated, 'You poor boy!'

She shoved the lot into his hands.

'Off you go, now. But you must promise to call in on me sometime soon, to give me news. You will, won't you?'

Fondly, like a child, she kissed the tips of her fingers, then gave him a little pat on the cheek. 'Off you go!'

For he was standing there, rooted to the spot, looking so stunned that she burst out laughing.

'You're just a poor little kid . . . my poor pet.'

Linette was not asleep, and her eyes welcomed him as he came into the room, which already smelt like a sick-room.

'I hope, at least, that you weren't thinking of sending a telegram to Poitiers?'

'No, of course not.'

'Promise me you won't, whatever happens. What have you got there?'

'Grapes . . . and some dates. . . .'

'Foolish extravagance! All I want is a drink.'

Her complexion was yellow, and her forehead ominously bathed in perspiration. Somewhere in the hotel, someone was sweeping the carpets with a vacuum cleaner.

'Did you get the money?'

'Yes, of course. You mustn't let it worry you. They've promised to let me have as much as I need.'

She was not reassured. She too, like his mother, did not trust him.

'The League, you mean?'

'The Major was very decent about it.'

'You'll have to be careful, all the same, Gérard . . . I know you. . . .'

Everyone knew him! Even the Major knew him! No one trusted him. No one took him seriously.

Even Pilar thought him a bit of a joke. Laughing, and showing the tips of her little white teeth, she had murmured pityingly, 'You're just a poor, helpless baby.'

His head was swimming from exhaustion, from nervous tension. And the drink he had taken earlier in the day, to raise his spirits, had only made him feel sick.

V

Pilar was the first to arrive at the appointed meeting-place. She was waiting for him on the corner of the Avenue de Wagram and the Place de l'Etoile. She was extremely smartly dressed, wearing very high-heeled shoes, and a red hat that blazed in the dazzling sunshine.

Why was it that fate seemed always to withhold her favours from him? He caught sight of her when there were still some twenty paces between them, but she had not seen him coming. Even when she was quite alone, she still smiled to herself, as if her thoughts were never anything but agreeable. The same could be said of almost everyone in the streets that day, men and women, perhaps on account of the glorious spring weather, or perhaps because of the time of day, for those who are at leisure at five o'clock in the afternoon do not have the same worries as those who are shut up in offices, factories and shops until six, when they join the milling crowds that throng the Metro stations.

The Arc de Triomphe bathed in sunlight, Pilar waiting for him like some pretty, expensive toy, and, above all, just being there, instead of bent over his desk on the premises of the League, with his pen scratching over the surface of those loathsome envelopes. All little things, and yet they were enough to make him feel that he was walking in a world of dreams.

She had seen him, and it gave him a thrill of pleasure, because he had been so often a mere envious onlooker at such meetings between a man and a woman on this very spot in the Place de l'Etoile. And now it was he who was being greeted by a pair of kindly, laughing eyes, he who could feel an arm being slipped into his.

'Am I late?' he said.

'No . . . let's go.'

He had waited deliberately until a quarter to five, before asking Drouin, 'Do you mind if I slip out for a moment, to see if my wife needs anything?'

And, as foreseen, Drouin had taken out his watch, and sprung it open.

'You needn't bother to come back this evening.'

Then he had bounded along the Rue de l'Etoile. Sitting up in bed, Linette was knitting some small garment for the baby. She had lost all track of time.

'Back already?'

'I'm on my way to do the rounds of the newspapers. I just thought I'd look in on my way to say hello.'

He was suddenly seized with panic. It had not occurred to him until now that he ought to be carrying a bundle of some fifty envelopes. His wife might have noticed that his pockets were empty. Hastily, he bent over and kissed her on the forehead.

'How are you feeling?'

'Fine.'

She was much better. She still had a temperature, but now the doctor came to see her only every other day.

'Is there anything you want? Would you like me to bring you something nice to eat?'

'You're so good to me.'

It was he who, a few days ago, had bought her the pink wool and knitting needles. It was he, also, who got up at six in the morning to do the housework, because Linette was unhappy at the neglected state of the room. And, seeing that his wife was still strictly confined to bed, he sponged her down every day with warm water.

'See you later.'

He fled. Now, he was walking arm in arm with Pilar.

'I wasn't really sure you'd come. You're such a strange boy.'

It was she who had made all the running. It was she who, having found out the times when he went back to his hotel to look after his wife, had loitered, looking out for him, on the corner of the Avenue de Wagram and the Rue de l'Etoile. At the beginning, he had seemed almost scared, but by now he was used to her.

'Let's have a look at you.'

She stood in front of him, straightened the knot of his tie, and refolded the blue pocket-handkerchief that she had given him.

'You can tell your wife it's a present from someone at the League.'

She loved giving presents: oranges and sweets for Linette, whom she had never seen, handkerchiefs and Virginia cigarettes for him. At this very moment she was slipping another packet into his pocket. Then, just as they were approaching Le Florida, she slipped something else into his pocket. He caught a glimpse of it as she did so, and recognized it as a hundred-franc note, folded very small. She squeezed his arm affectionately, silently begging him to accept it.

'It's to pay for the drinks . . . yes . . . I insist . . . not another word.'

It was not vouchsafed to him, it seemed, to enjoy his rare pleasures unalloyed. This gesture of hers had already cast a shadow. And yet, it could not be avoided. He had been worrying, only a moment ago, about whether he had enough money to pay for their drinks.

Le Florida was in the Avenue Macmahon. A doorman in uniform, a deep-piled carpet, a longish corridor where the electric light, combined with the sunshine, cast mysterious shadows. Pilar drew aside a curtain.

72

And, all of a sudden, his whole life, everything he had ever known, seemed very far away. They had entered a world so foreign to his experience that he had scarcely dreamed of its existence. At first he had difficulty in adjusting his vision to the dimness around him, for the lighting was very subdued. The colour scheme was muted, walls, carpets and furniture were in old rose or mole-grey, the band was also muted, and there were a few couples revolving slowly on the dance floor, so slowly that they sometimes seemed fixed like figures in a frieze.

Pilar, very much at home, exchanged greetings with several young men, nearly all of whom she addressed by their first names.

'Good evening, Nic. . . . Hello, Jean-Pierre. . . . All alone?'

Mindful of her companion's lack of self-confidence, she guided him discreetly.

'Look, over in the corner, there. That should suit us nicely.'

On the way to the table, she had had time to take note of all those present.

'He's not here . . .' she remarked.

And, sinking back into a low armchair, she crossed her legs.

A waiter in evening dress came up to them.

'Two pink gins, Fred,' she ordered.

Needless to say, the man's first reaction to him was hostile, because he was a newcomer, an outsider and, as he was keenly aware, unsophisticated. She looked at him, and burst out laughing.

'Why the scowl, darling?'

He knew that such places existed, but to know of something and suddenly to find oneself face to face with it were two very different things. Here, in the middle of the afternoon, at a time when he should still have been in his office waiting patiently for six o'clock, or taking letters and parcels to the post office in the Rue Balzac, while thousands and thousands of people were at work in offices and factories, there were twenty or maybe thirty young men, smartly dressed, looking so fresh that they might just have got out of a bath, and with nothing better to do than drink, smoke cigarettes, and flirt with pretty women.

'Don't you like it?'

'Do you come here often?' he asked, jealously.

'Whenever I have nothing better to do.'

A man in a dinner jacket, a mulatto, with a disdainful smile, was passing their table. She called out to him, 'Hello, Bobby! Isn't the boss here this evening?'

He pointed to a little door.

'Alone?'

'He's engaged at the moment, but it won't take long.'

'Can you give me a light? Thanks.'

Nonchalantly he lit her cigarette with a handsome gold lighter. She explained to Gérard, 'He's in the garden . . . . There's a garden out there, though you wouldn't think so. He's an odd fish, you'll see, Do you dance?'

They danced, and this was yet another disappointment. He had prided himself on being a good dancer, but from the beginning he could feel that his partner was controlling him. Very discreetly, as if unintentionally, she was leading him.

'Take it slowly . . . like this . . . do you see?'

And, seeing him stiffen, she said, 'Have I offended you?'

'No.'

'What you must do is glide, just glide. No hopping about.'

And so it was, always. He was a victim in a hostile world. Why was he so different from other people? Why could he never do anything right? They returned to their table.

'You have the makings of a very good dancer. Yes, I mean it. I'll teach you. . . .'

74

Just as she had had to teach him how to kiss, and even how to make love. Just as she had had to show him how to knot his tie, and arrange his handkerchief in his pocket, so that only the tip was left showing.

'You're such an odd boy. Now you're cross with me again.'

'Nonsense!'

And besides, he might have pointed out that she herself was somewhat out of place in these surroundings. Little as he knew of such things, he could see that Pilar was different from most of the other women present. But would he have recognized the difference, had she not told him that some months ago she had worked as a maid for a Spanish diplomat in the Avenue Hoche?

'Above all, don't let yourself be intimidated by Monsieur Duhour. He has rather a frigid manner, but actually it's only a pose he adopts to impress people. . . . In fact . . .'

He broke in aggressively, 'Have you slept with him?'

She shrugged, and looked around, as though making an inventory of the other women present.

'If you ask me,' she said, 'there aren't three women here – and I include society women – who haven't. . . .'

A young man came up to them, and asked Pilar to dance. Gérard had never seen anyone dance like that. The couples evinced no sense of elation – and surely elation was what dancing was all about? – but rather the reverse, it was as if they were deliberately avoiding it. They seemed scarcely to be moving, just inching their way around the floor, their expressions at once grave and smiling, smiling with restraint, as if engaged in some mysterious ritual, which afforded them covertly voluptuous delights.

It was pleasant, sitting there in his comfortable armchair, and yet twice he very nearly got up and left.

Someone came in through the little door.

On her return to their table, Pilar announced, 'He must be alone now. Come. What are you looking like that for?'

75

Like a man surrounded by enemies, preparing to take on the lot single-handed! The door opened on to a sunny garden enclosed by high walls, with a single tree in the middle, a large chestnut, just coming into flower. Under this tree was a green table, on which stood a bottle and two glasses. A man of between fifty-five and sixty, dressed in black, with a very white face, was seated at the table, smoking a cigar.

He watched them coming towards him, showing no surprise. He examined Gérard from head to foot, and, as he stood facing him, Gérard felt that the man had learned everything there was to know about him.

'Good evening, Monsieur Duhour. I hope I'm not intruding?'

'Good evening, my dear.'

'May I take the liberty of introducing my good friend, Gérard Auvinet?'

She also realized that he had sized him up, and understood everything. He had not risen from his chair, but contented himself with taking the girl's hand in his for a moment, and stroking it. Then he pointed to two metal chairs.

'Sit down, young man.'

He was dressed as soberly as a lawyer, but he was entirely lacking in any sense of style. His collar was grubby, and he was wearing a celluloid dickie with a tie attached.

'My friend is employed for the present as secretary to Jean Sabin.'

Cold and expressionless his face might be, but his grey eyes sparkled with malicious amusement.

'Oh! So you're with that outfit!'

And he added, almost with a wink, 'A shrewd bunch, what? But their staff have to work for peanuts. What are they paying you?'

So he had seen through that fairy-tale about Gérard's being the novelist's secretary. He knew. He knew all about the League. There was no point in lying to him.

'Eight hundred francs.'

76

Was there a hint almost of respect in those laughing eyes? His glance rested for an instant on the young man's left hand.

'And you're married . . . . How old are you?'

'Twenty.'

Duhour exchanged a knowing glance with Pilar. It was clear that those two understood one another.

'How many months have you been in Paris?'

Months he had said. How did he know that Gérard had not been here for years?

'Just over four months.'

'What part of the country do you come from?'

'Poitiers.'

'I used to know someone there. I knew him very well, name of Bonte, the head of a law firm.'

The firm of Bonte! The very firm where Monsieur Coutant, who had been one of the witnesses at their marriage, was employed.

'What a scoundrel!'

And the word, on his blanched lips, sounded like a compliment.

'So, to get down to business, you're looking for a job, any job?'

It was Pilar who replied on his behalf.

'He's not suited to his present job with the League. They're just exploiting him. He's intelligent, well-educated. . . .'

'What school?'

In the presence of such a man, Gérard was incapable of telling a lie. He began, 'The *Lycée* . . .'

Then, in spite of himself, 'Up to the third year . . . . When my father died. . . .'

But of course! This man had already seen right through him. He had even noted Auvinet's socks, those socks that he had bought yesterday evening in one of the big stores, saying, as he showed them to his wife, 'You must agree that

77

they look exactly like real silk. They only cost six francs fifty, but no one could possibly tell.'

It seemed, however, that he had been mistaken. Monsieur Duhour had not been taken in.

'He's here at my insistence, Monsieur Duhour. I explained to him that Le Florida was only one of your many business interests. I told him about your club, your chain of casinos in Normandy and on the Riviera. . . .'

He held up a warning hand, as a hint that Gérard should not pitch his hopes too high.

'What languages do you speak?'

'I learnt English at school.'

'But you don't speak it! And you have a wife who would expect to follow you everywhere.'

'Not necessarily.'

'What do you mean?'

And, once again, he exchanged glances with Pilar. It was as if he were saying, Did you hear that? He's even ready to ditch his wife!

Too bad! He could ditch her without actually abandoning her! He was so desperate to get away from the League and try his luck elsewhere that, coward that he was, he stammered, 'My wife and I are more like good friends. She understands perfectly that I have my future to consider. . . .'

And Duhour retorted, sardonically, albeit in a kindly tone, 'In other words, she would agree to go home to her parents?'

'Perhaps not to her parents. . . .'

Unprepared for all these questions, he was forced to improvise, 'She's expecting a baby. She's in poor health. I might be able to find somewhere for her in the country.'

If it was necessary, that's what he would do. His mind was made up. There was nothing he would not do if he had to.

'Does he dance?' the man asked Pilar.

And she replied, 'He can learn.'

'Listen to me, you two. I'm not prepared to make any promises, just like that, on the spur of the moment. You'll have to come and see me again . . . but not too soon. It's in the summer that I mostly take on extra staff, for the casinos. If he was a barman or a head waiter, there'd be no problem.'

Then, looking Gérard straight in the eye, he asked yet another question, 'Do you play poker?'

'I . . . yes . . . a little. . . .'

'Right. You don't play poker.'

He stood up and re-lit his cigar, which had gone out.

'At any rate, don't be in too much of a hurry to give up your job with the League . . . that bunch has connections. I know a boy who used to work for them, and he managed to worm himself into a job with a local government official. Now there's someone who knows what he wants, and won't rest until he gets it.'

He left them. So he knew Malterne, he was well-informed about him. Maybe he even knew that Malterne had dipped his hand in the till!

They returned to the dance hall, where they finished their drinks.

'You mustn't lose heart. He'll find you something, I'm sure. He's always like that . . . he enjoys putting people down.'

He did not demur, but he felt very bitter. Monsieur Duhour's manner was almost as discouraging as the Major's. It was as if the pair of them knew him better than he knew himself.

'Another of those!' they seemed to be saying.

Another of those, another of that sort, another young man, a penniless young man, with no useful connections, no special qualifications, who had come to Paris dreaming of making his fortune.

He began to wonder whether it was his age that was against him, and he was beginning to feel ashamed of it himself. Yes, he hated being so young. It was nothing but a handicap, which brought him humiliation at every turn.

'Go on, pay!'

Ah! yes, with the hundred francs she had slipped into his pocket! He paid, and followed her into the street. It was not yet dark.

'Are you going back home?'

'I must. My wife needs me.'

'You don't look too happy. Don't worry, he'll look after you, take my word for it.'

'I know, I know!'

'Come on, let's see you smile.'

'There.'

'And a kiss.'

She put up her cheek, and he brushed his lips against it.

'Do you do the cooking for your wife?'

She could feel that it would be wiser not to labour the point, to let him alone. But she couldn't resist teasing him a little, just once more, 'Tomorrow! Promise! Otherwise I'll come and fetch you at your wife's!'

And then she was off, prancing along the street, bubbling over with life and gaiety.

From the dairy he bought mashed potatoes and cooked vegetables, and then he went into the pork-butcher's for a sliver of lean ham. He went up the hotel stairs with a heavy tread.

'Back already?'

She was still sitting up, quietly knitting in the dusk.

'Have you finished your rounds?'

'Yes.'

He lit the stove and warmed up the food. When they had eaten, he washed up the two plates and the cutlery in the handbasin. He tidied the room, toyed for a little while with the idea of going out, then at nine o'clock, though he was not in the least sleepy, went to bed.

He had a bad night. For hours he lay dozing, not fully

awake and yet not really asleep, tormented by his thoughts, which were exaggeratedly, even unhealthily, gloomy.

First it was the socks, which Monsieur Duhour had stared at with a look almost of pity. And this led on to the little lecture in Vannier's study. Vannier, too, had looked him up and down with critical appraisal, and had impressed upon him the importance of going to a good tailor.

Pilar had taught him how to knot his tie. Earlier this evening she had endeavoured to teach him to dance.

When it came down to it, what was he fit for? He had nothing to offer. He couldn't even speak English! That was what they were all trying to tell him with their pitying looks, though not in so many words.

'It's very creditable to strive for success, but what at?'

He was a good-for-nothing. His mother had been right when she had said, 'The best thing for you would be to get a job with the railways, or in the Civil Service. That way, you'd have security for the rest of your life.'

And, come to think of it, what was it that had deterred him? Perhaps it was not ambition? Was he genuinely ambitious? Perhaps it would be nearer the truth to say that he was scared. But scared of what?

Of Sundays in a provincial town, for one thing. He had a vivid recollection of what it was like on Sundays in his own district or in the town centre: the almost deserted streets, with dim figures who seemed to cast no shadows, going God knows where. And the office workers, stiff in their best clothes, with their wives all dressed up, strolling along, pushing a pram, or leading children by the hand.

Why did all this torment him to such a pitch that he wanted to scream? And the dusky evenings in the empty streets, the lighted windows of the little local shops, and the men returning home, pausing to take their keys out of their pockets, and solemnly inserting them into the keyholes.

It was fear that had prompted his first attempt at escape, when he had enlisted in the army.

He felt hot. His wife was still running a temperature, and, because she still had to spend the whole day in bed, the sheets were damp. He moved away from her, closer to the wall, and willed himself to fall asleep, but unhappy memories kept crowding in thick and fast.

Horses, for instance. He was terrified of horses. It had been his own choice, a gesture of bravado, of pride, that had prompted him to join the cavalry. And from the very first, in the stables, at exercise, he had been so frightened of the horses that at night, in bed, he had run a temperature.

He could not conquer his fear. At exercise, he had felt an irresistible impulse to fling himself out of the saddle. And he had done so. He had been to see the Medical Officer, and pretended that he had fractured his leg as a child, that it was still causing him considerable pain.

He was excused all equestrian duties, and instead, cringing with shame, he was put on fatigues. For two months, the two most awful months of his life, he had moved heaven and earth to get transferred to office work.

Already he was marked down as a misfit, and he would never be anything else. He felt ashamed of his uniform, which did not fit. He could not recall how many times he had swapped tunics with other men in his barracks, even offering to pay for the privilege, but each tunic was a worse fit than the one before, and the last one was so tight on him that he looked like a female music-hall artiste in drag.

Almost every night, he would fall asleep feeling ashamed of himself. Ashamed of the trivial sums, two francs, one franc fifty, that he nicked every day from the petty cash at the League. Ashamed of his letters to his mother, full of promises and lies, ashamed of doing nothing for her, although he knew – who better? – the miserable conditions of her life in Poitiers.

He so longed to think well of himself! His intentions were always good, even admirable. Had he not done the right thing by Linette, without a moment's hesitation? Hadn't he

82

always shown himself loving towards her? Hadn't he done everything he possibly could to take care of her to the best of his ability, to such an extent, in fact, that of late he had had practically no sleep?

People in general would have one believe that youth is a treasure beyond compare, but when one is young oneself, the whole world seems to hold it against one, or else treat one with smiling condescension.

He was not to blame for his petty thieving. He was forced into it. Money! Always money! That hateful commodity which had been a stumbling-block to him all his life! Even at school, when his companions . . .

He recalled Le Florida, and all those young men, scarcely older than himself, in good suits, drinking cocktails at the bar, addressing the women by the familiar *tu*, taking gold or silver cigarette cases from their pockets.

He fell asleep at last, the corners of his mouth drooping miserably, and tears glistening on his eyelashes. If only he were a baby, to be rocked in someone's arms, to be comforted with soothing words, and above all to be protected from harm; but life was not like that. It was every man for himself, alone.

Even Pilar . . . . At first he had not wanted ever to see her again, because she too frightened him. He was still afraid of her. God knows where she was leading him. And he shuddered to think of the complications, once Linette was up and about again!

He slept for a while, woke at three in the morning, and took advantage of this to give his wife her medicine.

'Oh! Gérard, you poor dear, what a burden I am to you.'

'Nonsense. It's only natural. . . .'

He was standing barefoot on the cold floorboards. He got back into bed, mulling over a suggestion put to him by Mademoiselle Berthe.

Now there was someone really at peace with herself. She was serene, content with her lot, content just to be alive.

83

She went about her business, clean, unobtrusive, conscientious, tolerant and ever smiling. Every night, she went home to her old mother, who was a herbalist, with a shop in the Rue de Picpus. He could picture her surrounded by the acrid aroma of dried herbs.

Might it not be an idea to seek help from Dufayel's?

He was still thinking of this when he awoke. He lit the spirit-stove, put the water on to boil, shaved, and did the daily chores, which by now had become a habit. Lying with her head on the pillow, his wife kept an eye on him, from time to time reminding him of small things left undone.

'I wonder if we'll ever have a place of our own, with everything clean and new?'

She had a horror of dirt, even of dinginess. The bed, in which so many strangers had slept before them, filled her with disgust, as did the dark curtains, the stained rugs, and the armchair which had doubtless been used by any number of old men making love to naked young girls.

Her hopes for the future centred on a flat or a small house, very neat and tidy, with pretty furniture, new furniture, and later perhaps a maid, immaculate household linen, nice clothes: a wool coat with a fur collar, and long sessions at the milliner's . . . and good china to bring out when friends came to tea. . . .

How could she possibly understand that this prospect, too, frightened him? It would have been pointless to try and explain. He could picture a setting, a way of life. There it was, a house, a street or an office. And all of a sudden it would freeze, becoming nothing more than a still photograph, in which everything – people and objects – was fixed for all eternity. He would feel trapped in an invisible prison, and the anguish of it would rise in his throat like bile, making him long to struggle against his bonds, to escape, shouting 'No! No!' in his distress.

'Don't forget to buy some spirit for the stove. There's hardly any left in the bottle.'

He went out to do the shopping. The streets were almost deserted. The green street-cleaning vans were out, moving slowly, and sprinkling the roads with ribbons of fresh, gleaming water.

What was the most he could ask for? Two thousand francs? Better to ask too much than too little. The worst was having to beg another favour of the Major. But this time it was not money he wanted, merely his signature.

He set out the medicines, the water, the spirit stove, everything else she might need, on the bedside table.

'What's your temperature?'

'Not much above normal.'

'I've hung a clean towel over the back of the chair, in case the doctor comes while I'm out.'

It took him eight days. It was a great deal more complicated than he had expected. He took time off, on the pretext that he had things to do for his wife, and hastily dashed off to take the Metro to Dufayel's, on the corner of the Boulevard Barbès. Right at the top of the building, there were innumerable barred reception counters, all with long queues in front of them. He was among his own kind here all right. He knew all the signs, the threadbare, shabby clothes, the furtive glances, the outbursts of irritability.

He was given a form to fill in: Age. Occupation. Marital status. Number of children (if any). Name and address of parents. Present salary. Furnished or unfurnished accommodation. Amount of loan required. Is some of the money to be spent at Dufayel stores, or any of the others listed below? Repayment by monthly or weekly instalments? In either case, how much? Guarantors.

He wrote in the names of Jean Sabin and the Major.

Very good. Now all he needed was their signatures. He would also have to put down a third of the money himself, and finally he would have to wait several days until investigations were completed.

Better to drop the whole thing. The notion of an investigation into his affairs terrified him.

Nevertheless, his eyelids drooping and his eyes glazed, he went upstairs to see the Major at the end of the day.

'Please forgive me, Major.'

He was always asking people to forgive him. It had been drummed into him by his mother. Always sound apologetic and self-effacing. That was the way a well brought up young man should behave.

'As you know, we are expecting a child very soon. It occurred to us, my wife and me, that we ought to be looking out for a place of our own . . . . Anything unfurnished would be cheaper than the hotel. . . .'

The Major looked at him, as if to say, 'Of course, yes . . . I understand.'

And he went on endlessly, explaining, elaborating, running on at great speed, like someone who keeps going for fear of falling down if he stops.

'I approached Dufayel's for a loan, to enable me to buy the bare necessities. They asked for guarantors.'

The Major held out his hand, perfectly prepared to sign. What was the point of talking at such great length? It was probably not the first such request he had received. Perhaps Bigois?

He flushed at the thought.

'I give you my word that I won't get into arrears with the repayments. And besides, you have my salary as security.'

He was forgetting that he had already been paid two months in advance.

'I have also taken the liberty of naming Monsieur Jean Sabin.'

'Leave it with me.'

And next morning, the Major, as he was passing Gérard's desk, put down the form, now bearing the two signatures. Probably he did not mean to seem contemptuous. All the same, it had brought a flush to Gérard's cheeks, and he was minded to proceed no further in the matter.

The more so, since there was no way he could pay the deposit, a third of the total amount of the loan! And he would have to tell Linette. More evasions, more lies. Every day of his life! In a sense, every minute of his life was a lie.

He toyed briefly with the idea of asking Pilar for help, but quickly dismissed it as shameful and cowardly.

'Listen, Linette. . . .'

She was all too familiar with this opening. She was at once on her guard, sensing trouble ahead. She mistrusted him, just like his mother.

'You remember that fellow I told you I met the other night?'

The night of his first meeting with Pilar, when he had come home at one in the morning. He had told her that he had met someone in the little café in the Avenue des Ternes, and they had got into conversation, a man who knew his way around, who might be able . . . who . . .

'I've seen him again since. He wants to introduce me to someone influential, a retired solicitor or notary, I'm not quite sure which, who owns a whole chain of casinos . . . . D'you understand?'

This was another sign that he felt ill-at-ease. However, his wife knew by now that if, by some ill-chosen word, she were to provoke him, there would be the usual scene, tears, hysterics, beating the wall with his fists, leading in the end to her having to comfort him like a child.

'The trouble is, I don't want to go and see him wearing these clothes. I realize now that Vannier was right . . . . Remember? "Clothes make the man", he said. The fact is, in Paris . . .'

He dreaded having to come to the point. As a wedding present, Linette's parents had given her a winter coat, made to measure by a local tailor. The material was of the best quality, very warm and cosy. It was a coat that would last for years, and could be improved, if necessary, by the addition of a fur collar.

'Here we are, with spring and summer ahead of us. By next year, I shall have found my feet . . . . You haven't lost confidence in me, I hope?'

And thus it was that he got his way.

'If you think . . .'

'I don't think, I'm sure, don't you see? I'm so sure that I shall succeed. . . .'

And he really meant it. All that was needed was a smart, three-piece suit, the real thing, like those worn by the young men who patronized Le Florida, and his whole life would undergo a transformation.

He folded the coat into a suitcase, and hurried off with it to a little back street behind the Crédit Municipal. He got three hundred francs for it. That left him only a hundred francs short. And Linette had a gold wrist-watch that she never wore.

Twice more he went back to Dufayel's, and on his third visit he left with two vouchers worth a thousand francs each in one pocket, and in the other the list of shops where he could obtain goods in exchange.

At last, the following day in his lunch hour, he emerged from a large clothing store in the town centre, wearing the smart suit he had, for so long, dreamed of possessing, easy-fitting, square-shouldered and narrow-waisted. Now, all that was needed to complete the outfit were shoes, socks and a hat to match the suit. The whole transaction took him barely half an hour. He felt like a new man, so much so that he almost decided to hail a taxi. Instead, however, he went into a delicatessen, and bought expensive delicacies, rounds of *foie gras*, some smoked salmon, and a mayonnaise salad.

He peered covertly at the people around him, hoping against hope to be noticed, smiled at and admired.

It was not until he was going upstairs in the hotel that he

began to drag his feet. He felt awkward, apprehensive. Flinging open the door, he brandished his little parcels, and called out in a strained voice, 'Guess what I've brought you!'

And, feeling himself very close to tears, he forbore to add, Look, I'm only a kid, really. Is it my fault that I've had all the burdens of a grown man thrust upon me?

VI

This, he was well aware, was the most critical moment of his life. All the others seemed to realize it as well, his wife, the people at the League, and Monsieur Duhour, with his calculating expression. It was as if the word had gone round among them. No one made any attempt to hold him back. The mild spring weather, such as he had never known, seemed almost to be in collusion with them.

At the League, things had come to such a pass as to make him feel thoroughly ill-at-ease. For what, in actual fact, was he doing there, apart from collecting his salary? Always in advance, needless to say. The cleaning woman still lit the fire every morning, from habit, and because nobody had thought to tell her not to. But, as soon as they arrived in the office, they opened the windows. And that was enough totally to change the atmosphere.

From one moment to the next, they suddenly found themselves breathing the same sparkling air that permeated the Rue Daru, the Place des Ternes, the Avenue Hoche, and those imposing buildings, where servants could be seen at work, brushing suits and coats.

Drouin had taken to wearing a straw boater, and Mademoiselle Berthe a dark red straw hat.

'How is your wife?' one or other of them would enquire.

'Getting better all the time, thanks.'

And so she was. She was no longer in pain. Had it not been that she was still running a temperature, she would not have been obliged to stay indoors. He would have expected Linette to chafe at this, but not at all. Quite the reverse. He had bought her a quilted dressing-gown with what was left of the two thousand francs. It was made of cheap, artificial satin, a rather unattractive pale blue in colour. But it was padded, and that was all that mattered. She wore this dressing-gown from morning to night, with her feather-trimmed mules, and, sitting by the window, she would knit for hours at a stretch, without getting bored.

Formerly, she had been in the habit of asking him for an account of his activities, and in particular his expenditure. Money had been her main concern, because his propensity to spend more than he could afford was a worry to her. Now she had ceased to think about it. Perhaps, out of gratitude for his attentions during her illness, she pitied him for all the trouble she had caused him?

More probably, he suspected, it was her placid temperament that was reasserting itself.

She was happy, confined within four walls. She had been happy when confined to her bed. Sometimes, in the evening, she would let fall some small hint of her real preoccupations.

About the coat, for instance. Five or six days after he had sold her coat, she had suddenly said, 'I've had an idea. If things turn out for you as well as you expect . . . I mean, it wouldn't cost all that much more if you were to buy me a fur coat next winter . . . squirrel, perhaps . . . . A fur coat lasts for years and years, almost a lifetime, in fact.'

When she used to fret over him, he was irritated. And now, when she left him to his own devices, he resented her indifference. The truth was that he resented the lot of them for failing to hold him back.

Another time, she said, 'I've been thinking over the question of a flat, and it seems to me that, in the long run, a small house in the suburbs would suit us better. For one thing, it's more homely . . . . And I've worked out a scheme. . . .'

She had actually gone to the lengths of drawing a plan, and sketching in the layout of the furniture.

At the League, there was no work for him to do. Quite literally, he did absolutely nothing. Admittedly, the others were not kept very busy either. Presumably, the League went to sleep in the spring, or was it that political life had come to a temporary halt? At any rate, circulars were no longer sent to the membership, or notices to the newspapers. There were few visitors.

Drouin spent his time reading weekly magazines, chiefly of the girlie type, or writing long letters to his girlfriends in his bold, schoolmasterly hand.

One morning, when Mademoiselle Berthe was upstairs with the Major, and Mademoiselle Lange happened to be coming in late because she had an appointment with her dressmaker, Jean Sabin had rung to ask for his mail. Gérard had gathered up the letters, knocked at the door, and as he was opening it, heard the novelist call out, in his resonant voice, 'Come in, my pretty.'

Jean Sabin, naked to the waist, wearing nothing but a pair of striped pyjama trousers, was engaged in shaving, right there in his office, standing at the open window, which overlooked a little garden. Then he realized that it was not his secretary who had opened the door.

'Come in, my boy . . . I thought you were Lange. . . .'

The divan, converted into a bed, had not been made. The office smelt strongly of soap and eau-de-cologne.

'How's your wife?'

'Much better, thanks.'

'How old is the child now?'

'It's not born yet.'

'Of course, I was forgetting . . . . Well, go on, boy, what is it?'

Gérard now understood why Mademoiselle Lange always turned very pale whenever the Great White Chief received a woman in his office, and also why there were times when she returned to theirs with red-rimmed eyes.

Twice, sometimes three times, a day, Gérard went out ostensibly to attend to his wife's needs, but it was now merely an excuse. Often, he did not even bother to go all the way to the Rue de l'Etoile. It was enough for him just to stand enjoying the sunshine in the Rue du Faubourg-Saint-Honoré, and then go and have a drink in the Place des Ternes.

On the dot of five, he would collect the mail from the box.

'I'm off to the post office. If it's very crowded, I may not come back this evening.'

The Major, who went out for lunch more and more frequently, seldom got back until well after three, and sometimes did not come back at all.

What was the point? They were all living on other people's money, or money that belonged to no one, according to how you looked at it. Their salaries came from all those small postal orders and banknotes that the Major took out of their envelopes and arranged in neat little piles.

And, in spite of having very few letters to post, Gérard always managed to pocket four or five francs a day from the petty cash, even though, if he had been asked to provide a detailed account of his expenses, he would have been unable to do so.

At five o'clock Pilar was waiting for him on the corner of the Place des Ternes, and they set off without delay, arm in arm, for the Boulevard de Courcelles.

At first she said nothing. He noticed that she seemed a little anxious, but it did not worry him. It was not until the previous night, as they were leaving Le Florida, that she had murmured, 'I have a favour to ask you.'

They had been back to Le Florida three times, ostensibly to see Duhour. But this was really only a pretext. Duhour barely acknowledged their presence. He would wave to them across the room, and later perhaps come over to their table.

'Everything all right with you?'

He must have noticed the change in Auvinet's style of dress, but he had made no comment.

'I'm convinced he has no intention of doing anything for me. I don't think he likes me,' Gérard had said to Pilar.

'No, of course not. It's obvious you don't understand him. It's just his manner. He hardly knows you yet. He's only just begun making his plans for the summer season. He owns cinemas at Lion-sur-Mer and Riva-Bella, and several other small seaside resorts. Sooner or later, he'll need someone to fill a vacancy at one of those places. He's sure to think of you then, and that will be that.'

In his heart, he knew that this was not true, but he pretended to believe her. It was like a game in which everyone concerned was at pains to avoid saying anything that might bring them face to face with reality.

'Listen, Gérard, my dear. I'll be frank with you. It's two weeks now since I saw the friend who looks after me. I've never mentioned him to you before, but I'm sure you must have realized . . . I've telephoned his house several times, only to be told that he's away on holiday. Now he's never gone on holiday before without letting me know. There's something wrong, I can feel it in my bones. . . .'

Now, as they approached the railings of the Parc Monceau, she came out with it.

'Could you possibly try and get to see him personally? All you have to say is that it's to do with insurance. It's possible that they'll be on their guard, and they won't leave you alone together. But if you do manage to see him privately, I want you to mention me to him. What you must say is . . .'

He did not protest. He felt humiliated, more deeply humiliated than ever before in his life, he who had such vast experience of humiliation. But, instead of protesting, he forced a good-humoured laugh, which more or less concealed the bitterness he felt.

'Fine! I understand. . . .'

'Believe me, I'm not asking this for my own sake. I don't have to look further than Le Florida to find myself another protector. It wouldn't take more than two or three days. It's for his sake, poor soul. He's a thoroughly good sort. A man who has worked all his life for his money. He has eight children, all married. He's a widower. He lives with one of his daughters, and she's already had at least a million from him as a dowry. She's the one who keeps a close watch on him, on behalf of the others as well as herself. Can you believe it, they even have him followed when he goes out? They dole out small sums to him, by way of pocket money. He has to resort to all kinds of tricks, like a schoolboy, to be able to visit me.'

She sat waiting for him on a bench in the Parc Monceau, while he went into a handsome building and approached the concierge.

'Could I see Monsieur Bienvenu?'

'His flat is on the first floor, but I don't think he's at home.'

The staircase was magnificent though rather dark, like a church, with stained glass windows. He rang the bell. A stern-looking butler, dressed from head to foot in black, opened the door, and looked at him in silence.

'Could I have a word with Monsieur Bienvenu? It's on important business, very urgent.'

'Monsieur Bienvenu is away at present. Would you care to speak to his daughter, Madame Dorange?'

'It's a personal matter. Could you tell me when Monsieur Bienvenu is expected back?'

'He's out of Paris, and will probably not return for several months. Monsieur is at one of his country estates.'

And the flunkey, looking him up and down just as Monsieur Duhour had done, seemed to be memorizing every detail of his appearance, his exaggeratedly square shoulders, his tie, his pink silk pocket-handkerchief.

'Could you give me his address?'

'If you write to him here, the letter will be forwarded.'

Pilar sprang to her feet as he came towards her.

'What did I tell you? *They've bundled him out of the way!*'

Indignantly, she launched into a long tirade, 'He's been dreading this for some time now. I should explain that he's no longer young. His daughters are scared stiff he'll spend all their inheritance, and are prepared to go to any length to keep him stashed away in the country. They own a château in Normandy, near Etretat, and a place at Cap D'Antibes. He wouldn't go to either of them of his own free will, not at any price. I've heard him talk about it, and the very idea reduced him to tears! Poor old man!

'There was talk of appointing an administrator. All sorts of things were said. There were insinuations that he wasn't quite right in the head. D'you see? They called in psychiatrists, without letting him know who they really were. So he talked and talked. . . .

'"I'm quite convinced", he used to say, "that they want to have me certified. They're plotting against me the whole time."'

'And he's not certifiable?'

'No more than you or me. Come. . . .'

'Where are we going?'

'I'm not sure yet. Let's just walk.'

She went on, as if talking to herself, 'I simply must find some way of paying my rent, or else I'll be put out in the street. I only have a hundred francs left in the world, and the last thing I want is to ask Duhour for money. Because once one is in debt to him . . . I wonder. . . .'

And then, abruptly, 'Have a look and see if we're being followed.'

They were walking down the Boulevard Malesherbes, and, as far as Gérard could see, there was no sinister figure

96

following behind them. And besides, he didn't believe the half of what she had told him.

'All the same, it had better be you who . . . . One never can be sure. Listen, Gérard, dear . . . . He's given me bits of jewellery from time to time . . . just small trinkets . . . I don't know what they're worth. . . .'

And she looked back over her shoulder two or three times before opening her bag, and taking out an emerald ring.

And still as if talking to herself, 'It might be a real stone, but it could be junk . . . . One would have to find out from a jeweller. There's one in the Rue Rambuteau, almost next door to the Crédit Municipal. I know they buy second-hand jewellery.'

'Give it to me!' he said gallantly, and slipped the ring into his pocket.

'Wait! I'd better explain. They won't hand you the money over the counter, just like that. It's against the law. You'll have to give them your address, and they'll send you a cheque or bring cash to your hotel. Would that be inconvenient for you?'

The answer that rose to his lips was, 'After what I've sunk to. . . .' but he did not say it aloud.

'Shall we take a taxi?'

A taxi with the roof down, why not? And bask in the glorious climax of the sunset.

'If they ask you where you got the ring, what will you say?'

'That it belongs to my wife. After all, she has as much right as any other woman to have jewellery, don't you think?'

She persisted, 'True! Are you sure you don't mind?'

What she really meant, he knew, was, 'Aren't you a little scared?'

Oh! yes, he was scared all right, but what the hell! It was all their fault, the lot of them. Even including his mother, who, mollified by his most recent letter, had begged him to forgive her for having lost confidence in him. She had promised to wait a while before looking for a job as a servant, and to be less mistrustful of him in future.

They stopped the taxi on a corner, and mingled with the dense crowds on the narrow pavements. It was nearly six o'clock. They would have to hurry, or the shop would be shut. They peered through the window, past the display of jewellery, into the shop.

Pilar was on edge. Her hand tightened on her companion's arm. She appeared hesitant, as if on the point of abandoning the whole project.

'There is someone . . . . Let's walk on a bit. . . .'

There were shoppers everywhere. They retraced their steps, peering in at the faces of the salesmen.

'How does this one strike you?'

A youngish man, already somewhat overweight, was showing a customer out. His glance rested on them.

'I'm going in.'

He went in without further delay, and took the ring from his pocket.

'Good evening, Monsieur. I should be greatly obliged if you would value this ring for me.'

Strive as he might, he could not contain his agitation. He caught sight of himself in a mirror, and stiffened.

'It was a present to my wife from her aunt, and as, for the moment, she has no occasion to wear it . . .'

He felt his words to be absurdly ill-chosen, but it was too late. The man, having examined the emerald, had taken it to the door to look at it in daylight.

'Are you thinking of selling it?'

'That depends, naturally, on what you would offer me for it.'

'Have you any idea of its value?'

'Seeing that it was a present, you understand. . . .'

He knew that the man was not deceived. For all his plumpness and his rosy cheeks, his manner was cold, almost glacial.

'I was wondering if the stone might be genuine.'

'It appears to be.'

'In that case?'

'Would you be prepared to leave it with me until tomorrow? It's hard to tell at a glance. . . .'

'Could you give me an approximate idea of its value?'

'If, on closer inspection, my initial impression is confirmed, I could probably offer you, say, twelve thousand. . . .'

He subjected him to a piercing scrutiny.

'There's just one thing. I must warn you that I can't pay you the money here. It's against police regulations.'

His gaze did not waver, and Gérard found himself blushing, as if he had been accused of theft. He immediately assumed a casual air, too casual.

'That's perfectly all right.'

'Then you'd better leave me your name and address. Tomorrow, or the day after. . . .'

'The thing is . . . it's rather urgent.'

This was not true. Pilar could wait forty-eight hours. But as far as he was concerned, he couldn't wait to have done with the whole business.

For a moment it looked as if the man were minded to hand him back the ring and pull down the shutters, for it was now already ten past six.

'If you could possibly make it tomorrow. . . .'

At long last the man opened his ledger.

'Your name, Monsieur?'

'Auvinet. Gérard Auvinet. Hotel de l'Etoile, Rue de l'Etoile.'

And then, speaking very rapidly, 'I'm never there except before nine in the morning, and between twelve and half-past one. There's no need to come up to my room. They'll send someone up for me from the desk. My wife is ill, and . . .'

A blunder! Surely the jeweller must have seen him in the street with Pilar?

She was waiting for him, some fifty yards further on, looking pale and feverish. He resented this. Was she determined to frighten him out of his wits?

'Well?'

'It's settled, or as good as . . . . Twelve thousand. He's sending me the money at my hotel.'

Suddenly, she was bubbling over with high spirits, but it was not quite her usual high spirits.

'What about having dinner together, just the two of us? Or is your wife expecting you home?'

He would think up some tale to tell her, anything, since nowadays she believed every word he said.

They strolled along the Grands Boulevards, and chose a rather good restaurant. It was Alsatian, with a long-necked green bottle in a champagne bucket on every table.

'I had a pretty good idea that it was genuine', Pilar was saying. 'It's not the only thing he gave me, either . . . . That was the way he was . . . like a kid . . . . He'd fish something out of his pocket, just like that, not even in a box, and say,

'"For you, my precious. Here, take it."

'And it seemed to make him so happy. Poor man! I wonder whether his daughters have packed him off to Normandy or the south . . . . He was so terrified. . . .'

'Look here. . . .'

'I'm listening. . . .'

'You don't think. . . ?'

She knew at once what he was trying to say.

'Are you suggesting he pinched the jewellery from his daughters? Well, what if he did? He had every right, surely, seeing he gave it to them in the first place?'

'Of course. . . .'

'The thought had crossed my mind . . . . The fact that they were not in boxes, and he handled them as if they were just bits of junk . . . I wish you could have seen the pleasure he got from giving them to me.'

He felt he could do with another bottle of wine.

'There's something I want you to do for me, Gérard my pet . . . but first I want you to swear that you won't refuse.'

He pretended he had no idea what it was all about.

'Why do you want me to swear?'

'Because.'

Her tone was wheedling. He hesitated, for the sake of appearances.

'Swear!'

'No!'

'Right then, I'm leaving.'

'Come on now, don't go!'

'Swear!'

'People are looking at us.'

'Swear!'

'Oh, very well, I swear! There! Now, what is it you want?'

'That money you'll be getting tomorrow . . . . It's for both of us . . . . Yes! I insist . . . . Otherwise, I'll never be able to ask for your help again . . . . And there are other things . . . . You'll see. . . .'

He drank a great deal that night. Fortunately, he had a little money in his pocket. He dreaded going back to the hotel. He dragged Pilar from one place to another, always in search of bright lights, music and laughter.

She did not resist, fearful of angering him, although she was beginning to have a very good idea of how it would end.

'D'you realize it's midnight, darling?'

'What of it?'

'Your wife. . . .'

'My wife doesn't give a damn!'

He was in an ugly mood, his expression that of a man in revolt.

'Oh! yes . . . . If only you knew how little she cares whether I'm dead or alive . . . . No, not dead, because I haven't any life insurance yet. It's my duty, you see, to take out a life insurance policy. My father-in-law told me so. And, in the meantime, my wife keeps herself amused, making plans of her little house. Waiter!'

'What, another?'

'So now it's you trying to stop me drinking! That's a laugh, I must say. In fact, all life is nothing but a joke. You can't imagine how comical it all is! And look at all those bastards staring at us!'

He raised his voice, and, if he didn't watch out, she was fearful that it would end in a brawl.

'The world is crammed full of bastards. Take Jean Sabin, for instance, with his booming voice, his fat face, his monocle, puffing out his chest in the guise of a super-patriot! Some patriot! Oh! to be a patriot, don't you agree? Public speeches, processions, and a flogging for anyone less patriotic than himself.'

'Keep your voice down!'

'The hell, I will! If he was here, standing in front of me, I'd tell him a thing or two . . . . He sleeps in his office at the League . . . . He gets all his own work done by the League. It's the League that pays his secretary, and, as if that wasn't enough, he sleeps with her. It's the League's money that . . .'

'What about moving on somewhere else?'

'You're scared. Yes! Don't pretend you're not. I've got eyes in my head. Okay, okay, let's go. . . .'

Outside in the street, unsteady on his feet, he bumped into a passer-by.

'I beg your pardon, Monsieur.'

Solemnly he raised his hat with a flourish, and then burst out laughing.

'Come to think of it, he was probably another of those bastards, the same as the Major, the same as Drouin . . . Drouin! Now there's a really detestable fellow. Always spick-and-span, well-scrubbed and polished, and always with his hand on his heart. Oh! yes, his hand on his heart, his big, generous heart. Because, you see, he's one of those splendid, big-hearted fellows – you know the type – and I dare say he'll end up as a deputy. And then there's Bigois, the little bastard, definitely a bastard, but small fry. You don't know Bigois, do you? Listen to this, it's a hoot! He was shown the door because he was caught pilfering money from the envelopes. Because, you see, the envelopes are sacred. Oh, yes. Only the Major and Sabin have the right to help themselves to the member's contributions . . . . As for your Monsieur Duhour, now there's a man. . . .'

They ended up in the little café in the Place des Ternes, where Gérard insisted on having one last drink before going home. His hand being unsteady, he spilt it, ordered another, and burst into tears.

'Admittedly, if I've come to recognize a bastard when I meet one, it's because I'm a bastard myself. Oh! yes I am. Don't you dare contradict me. And besides, you think so too. Your offer just now to share with me proves it. So what am I, eh? A poor little bastard. Very small fry, admittedly. Ask your precious Duhour what he's thinking, when he looks at me with those cold fish-eyes of his. And to think that, all this while, my poor mother is stranded there, all on her own . . . . You don't know my mother, you see . . . . You never met my father. . . .'

'You're making a spectacle of yourself, Gérard!'

'To hell with that! Waiter, a drink! . . . . That's better.'

He went out, leaving his hat on the table. It did not occur to Pilar to retrieve it.

As soon as he got home, he was sick. Linette was obliged to get out of bed.

'Don't worry about me! There's no need to worry, I tell you. I don't have to tell you that, when you really come down to it. We deserve each other. True or not, my dear wife? Go on, say something.'

Shouting fit to wake the whole hotel, he repeated, 'My wife! My wife! My wife!'

And after a loud, mournful burst of laughter, he fell into a heavy sleep.

It must be assumed that, in spite of his torpor, his senses were alert, for he had not slept many hours when he became aware that something was going on. He opened his eyes, saw that the room was already bathed in sunlight, and that Linette was talking to a chambermaid at the half-open door.

'Send him up,' Linette was saying.

He leapt out of bed. He had a frightful headache, but he disregarded it.

'No! I'll go down.'

The maid hesitated, uncertain what to do.

'Go and tell him I'll be down in a minute.'

He put on his trousers and jacket, and smoothed his hair.

'Who is it?' asked his wife.

'I'll tell you later.'

On his way downstairs, he was seized with panic, so much aggravated by his hangover that he thought he was going to faint.

Had the jeweller been to the police? Could one be sure that the old man's daughters had not already reported the loss of the jewellery? He paused on the first-floor landing, his legs buckling under him, then, white as a sheet and shivering, he went down the last few steps.

'There's a gentleman to see you in the office.'

Only a few more paces to the door. It was not the police, but the salesman of the previous day, wearing an unbecoming, light brown, spring overcoat. On the wall, a

Westminster chiming clock, an exact replica of the one in the room where his wedding breakfast had taken place, began striking nine o'clock.

'I've come about your emerald ring.'

Gérard endeavoured, without much success, to smile.

'It was perhaps somewhat ill-considered on my part yesterday to mention the figure of twelve thousand. On reflection, I'm afraid the most I can offer you is ten . . . . In the circumstances, I thought it would be best to return the ring. . . .'

More complications! The last thing he wanted. Better to settle the matter there and then.

'So you haven't brought the money?'

'I have the money with me as well, of course. Now that I have checked your identity, there is no reason why . . .'

Gérard shrugged wearily, 'I'll take the money.'

'I have a receipt ready for you.'

Underneath the pigeon-holes for letters, there was a small bottle of violet ink and a pen with a scratchy nib. Glancing up at his own pigeon-hole, he saw that there was a letter from his mother-in-law.

He signed the receipt. The salesman counted out ten big thousand-franc notes. Gérard stuffed them into his pocket.

'Delighted to be of service. If, by any chance, you have other things . . .'

The hall porter had returned to his desk, leaving the office door open. Had there been time for him to see the money being handed over?

'Good day, Monsieur.'

He took his mother-in-law's letter from the pigeon-hole, hesitated, then went out into the street. He felt he needed a drink before going back upstairs. He was still wearing his slippers, and had not had time to put on a collar. He needed something, a glass of white wine, perhaps, to get rid of the foul taste in his mouth. He went into the nearest bar, only some twenty yards away, and, instead of white wine, decided in the end on something stronger.

'Who was it?' asked Linette.

'There's a letter from your mother . . . . Oh! you mean the man who called just now? You know that fellow I told you about, the one who thought he might be able to help me? The one who owns all those casinos. Well, he sent a messenger to say he wants me to go and see him. I bet you he's found me a job, something that will bring in more money right away.'

He could not show her the money yet. His head was spinning and aching terribly.

'Was it he you went out with last night?'

'Of course, who else?'

'A fine state he got you into! You should have warned him you have a weak head for drink. It's a good thing I'm feeling so much better. It won't be long now before I'm able to go out. And then I'll be able to look after you a little, you poor big baby.'

He had to blow his nose, which was sore. His eyelids were burning. He must have caught a cold.

'If you like, I'll send the maid to get us something for lunch.'

'There's no need. I've got plenty of time.'

Out in the street, he toyed with the idea of taking the day off from the League. He even considered the possibility of never going back. The building in the cul-de-sac suddenly filled him with revulsion. It reminded him of the un-reasoning revulsion he had felt in the banqueting room on his wedding day.

First, he must go to Pilar, and give her the money.

Then . . .

But then he remembered that he had had two months' salary in advance from the League. And then there was the business of the petty cash. How was he going to account for the discrepancies?

The whole town seemed to have been washed clean by the sunlight, and there was a fat woman pushing a little barrow piled high with flowers, accompanied by a small, bare-legged girl.

Everyone, all those who knew him at any rate, were in a conspiracy to let him have his head, to keep up the pretence that they took him for a grown man!

VII

Years and years later, there would from time to time emerge, from the dark nooks and crannies of his memory, shreds of painfully clear recollection of the events of this day, like grains of sand found in the pockets and seams of an old suit, recalling some long-past seaside holiday.

This bar, for instance, the bar where he habitually went for his morning coffee and croissants. Lost in thought, he went in automatically, then looked about him in surprise, not at first realizing what it was that struck him as out of the ordinary.

It was that it was past nine o'clock, and the long, red, copper, horseshoe-shaped counter was deserted, and a waiter, with a napkin tied round his neck, was polishing the percolator, while another, behind him, perched on top of a green ladder, was washing the front windows. Why should these things have remained so sharply etched in his memory when recalled in middle age, accompanied by that feeling of hazy confusion experienced when familiar objects assume a changed appearance?

His original intention had been to order coffee. His next thought was that it was well past breakfast-time. He had already drunk one glass of spirits. Why not another? But could he be sure that his queasy stomach could take it? He hesitated. He pondered the question, as if it were a problem of vital importance, then, after a long pause, ordered a half of beer, because he still had that foul taste in his mouth. And he continued to brood. It was an odd thing, this endless brooding. In one way, it resembled the skittering of mice in the corner of a room, in another, the sense of being tossed on a great wave, far more powerful than himself.

For everything that happened that day was founded on one thing, his decision to give up the struggle. At what point, precisely, had he made up his mind to this? Just now, only a few minutes ago perhaps, as he had left the hotel and walked along the Avenue de Wagram? Or perhaps later, when he had pushed open the door of the bar?

He had had enough of putting up a fight. All that was over and done with. Yes, of course, people would smile, if he were to tell them so. He alone knew, he alone would ever know, the savage intensity with which he had fought against circumstances.

Now he would let himself sink. He was sinking already. He had cut the life-line. He would let himself go, he would drift on the tide. Already, he felt relieved of a great burden, the more so because his head was swimming.

Had he not, in his heart, always known that he would be a failure? Had any of his schoolmates, or later the other adolescent youths of his generation, slouched about the streets as he had, with head bent, overcome by fits of dizziness?

Oh! he was perfectly lucid. He doubted whether he had ever been more lucid in his life. Take Linette, for instance. Had he not spent his time wandering the streets, he would never have married her, never have been haunted by the sight of those couples, huddled in dark corners, in winter especially, as he pictured cold hands, groping under warm outer garments, seeking the touch of moist flesh.

She had never understood. She used to say, 'Not here, for goodness sake!'

But elsewhere, in a real bedroom, in a real bed, he would have been less eager. It was in the street, on a night when a fine drizzle was falling, that the child had been conceived.

Once, some time just after his sixteenth birthday, he had had a presentiment of what the future held in store for him, or at any rate had become aware of the sort of woman who attracted him. A travelling vaudeville company had visited the town, including a troupe of young dancers. One of the dancers, the second on the right, had caught his eye. She had been paler, more sickly-looking than the rest, with a pinched face, the face of an undernourished child, in need of fresh air and sunshine.

He had sent her flowers. Clearly, the members of a troupe of that sort were not used to receiving flowers. The gesture had surprised everyone. He had returned that same evening, to see the show again, and afterwards had managed to find his way backstage.

'Was it you who sent me flowers? All the others are envious. They're wondering. . . .'

It was very cold and dirty in the wings. The costumes were worse than shabby. The company was leaving that night, and everyone had been helping to pack clothes and props in big wicker baskets. Some were eating sandwiches as they changed. His little dancer had taken his arm, and he had accompanied them to the station, only to learn that the train had been delayed, and was not expected until two in the morning.

The waiting rooms were locked. An icy wind swept the platform, where only a single light had been left burning. She had told him that her pay was twenty francs a day, less deductions, and that, to make matters worse, the former manager had made off with the takings.

And yet he had envied them, and her especially. Perhaps because she had also told him that she had a mother who was a streetwalker in Paris, and a drunken father who had gone off with another woman, and who, she believed, had served a term in prison.

He would give up the struggle. Maybe he should never have attempted it, battling on in the hope of becoming a man like any other, *the man his mother wanted him to be.* What did she know, poor, deprived woman that she was? She too was a victim, drifting towards God knows what end.

He felt an immense relief. He stood for a long while on the edge of the pavement, and, now that everything was settled, seemed to dwell with unwholesome relish on the small, practical problems of daily life.

Today differed from any other he had known, in that he was in the grip of two opposing forces. On the one hand, he was being swept along on a wave, a huge, turbulent, rising wave, against which he offered no resistance.

On the other hand, trivial little preoccupations nibbled away ceaselessly in his head, senseless, niggling worries. As at this moment.

Should he put in an appearance at the League before going to see Pilar, or leave it till later? As for the League, he had finished with it once and for all. On that his mind was made up. But he would not give in his notice there and then. He must, at least, make use of the money in his pocket to square his account. He was two months in arrears, at eight hundred francs a month, added to which were the small sums he had filched from the petty cash. In total, two thousand francs would set him right, and he could leave without a stain on his character.

It went against the grain to part with so much money. And besides, it seemed somehow indecent to spend any part of his share in the sale of the ring before giving Pilar what was due to her.

He lingered briefly outside a dairy. He felt a sudden longing for a piece of Roquefort cheese. He promised himself that he would buy some later. And some other sort of cheese for Linette, who did not like Roquefort, or indeed anything pungent.

He would go first to the League, just to put in an appearance. He would make some excuse, any excuse, otherwise there was the risk that they would send

Mademoiselle Berthe to enquire. Mademoiselle Berthe had already expressed anxiety over the possibility of a premature birth.

'If only you knew how common it is in Paris!'

'Why Paris, in particular?'

'Because of the Metro, and all the stairs, and the hustle and bustle of life. One sees it everywhere. The number of premature births. . . .'

And a good thing too. As he saw it, it would solve all their problems. Let the child come into the world today or tomorrow, it would afford him a good excuse vis-à-vis the League, and everyone else for that matter. What he would do about it was of no importance. He hadn't the least idea. The only thing that counted was that it would make a change . . . . Maybe, just for once, fate would be on his side.

Oddly enough, as he went into the offices of the League in the Impasse Daru, he had a premonition that it was for the last time. Passing Jean Sabin's door, he smiled sardonically. Then he went into his own office.

'Is the Major in?' he asked, not bothering to remove his hat, as if he were just passing through.

'He's gone to a funeral. He won't be coming in today.'

Too bad! All the better! He couldn't really tell.

'I just called in to let you know that I shan't be in to work for the next few days.'

'Your wife?' asked Mademoiselle Berthe, turning round.

He lied, without so much as a blush.

'Yes . . . . There seems to be some new development . . . . The doctor . . .'

And he was gone. How splendid if events were to bear out his lie! Such things do happen. It could easily happen to him.

He was free now to go to Pilar. He was free to do whatever he liked. He was free. He sauntered along the streets aimlessly, his hands in his pockets, his eyes screwed up against the sun, and then, God knows why, he stopped in front of the cinema, and gazed at the gaudy posters.

When he got to Pilar's flat, he had to knock several times, and even call out his name. She had still been in bed. He realized that she was coming, barefoot, to unbolt the door. Then he saw her running back to her divan, and burying herself in the bedclothes.

'Is it late?'

'I don't know.'

'Did he come?'

The bedroom was very light and cheerful. The red silk divan cushions were scattered about the floor, along with dresses and underwear. He drew the notes from his pocket, and flung them down on the sheets.

'He wouldn't give more than ten thousand. "Take it or leave it," he said.'

'Hand me my bag.'

She slipped five notes into it, and held out the rest. Then she said something that shocked him.

'Well, anyway, that's something his daughters won't get their hands on! When I think of those bitches . . . . What are you going to do now? Be a dear and switch on the hotplate. How's the hangover? Not too bad, I hope.'

He had not returned the money to his pocket. He would do so later, when her back was turned. She was using a lipstick that she had taken from her bag. Then she got out a compact, and powdered her nose. When she had finished, she rummaged in the bottom of the bag, and finally fished out a tiny key.

'Hand me that casket, over there on the dressing table.'

She unlocked it.

'Look. D'you see these earrings? If they turn out to be genuine too, they're probably worth even more than the ring. I never wear them. Can you imagine what they'd look like on me?'

The setting was old-fashioned, the sort of trinkets that are handed down from generation to generation.

'He was thrilled, just like a child, every time he managed

to bring me some bauble or other . . . . Looking very sly, he would hold out his closed fist, saying,

'"Are we going to say thank you to our sugar daddy?"'

The expression struck home. It shocked Gérard, and for an instant he could not look her in the face.

'Anything bulkier was more of a problem, d'you see. . . ? This jewel box, for instance . . . and the engraving hanging above the bed . . . . They watched him like a hawk . . . . What's the matter with you?'

'Nothing.'

Why was she talking to him like this, all of a sudden? Up to now she had been discretion itself on the subject, until last night, when she had put him in the picture. She had never conducted herself like a whore, and now, suddenly, her manner, even her tone of voice, revealed her in a light that shocked and appalled him.

It was as if she had made up her mind that henceforth she could let herself go with him.

More rings, a bracelet, an old, very heavy, silver cigarette case, with a monogram and a date engraved inside.

And now she was taking a little snapshot from the bottom of her bag. She held it out to him.

'Look.'

A pitiful old man, sixty-five years old at least, with heavy eyelids, a sunken mouth, and a troubled expression. One of those photographs so commonly seen in family albums.

'He's got such a kind face, don't you think? He was always so anxious not to cause me any inconvenience. He would knock at the door, and call out,

'"Can daddy come in?"'

At this, he suddenly stiffened, 'Shut up!'

She looked at him, surprised and displeased.

'What's come over you?'

'Nothing.'

A flicker of her habitual high spirits glinted in her eyes, and a smile spread over her face.

'Surely you're not jealous? Go on, tell me.'

'I said, shut up!'

'Really, it's too absurd! If I were to tell you how far he was past it, poor old soul!'

'No!'

'You're in a funny mood this morning. Come on, now, switch off the hotplate, and pour the water into the coffee pot.'

But he did not move.

'Are you sulking?'

He was not sulking. He was overcome with giddiness. He couldn't help himself. It seemed to him that he was seeing Pilar in an altogether new light. It was as if a harsh, pitiless arc lamp had been trained on her.

And, once again, a wave of panic flooded through his whole being.

'It's time I got up.'

He did not protest. He merely ignored her nakedness. The word that he had repeatedly uttered the previous night came back to him, 'Bastard.'

He muttered it under his breath, but today without anyone particular in mind.

'Is it because I told you about the old man? I don't see what right you have to get on your high horse, because . . .'

In her determination to put things right, she did something grossly offensive for the first time since he had known her. She picked up the money on the bed and slipped it into his pocket.

'Go on, smile, you great foolish boy! With all this loot, we're sitting pretty for a good while yet, and later on. . . .'

Not looking at her, he took the money out of his pocket and flung it on the bed.

'Have you gone out of your mind, or what? It must be some hangover, to make you carry on like an idiot.'

His head was spinning, spinning unbearably. His eyelids were burning. Was he going to break down and burst into tears? He wondered.

She went on talking, her Spanish accent exaggerating the vulgarity of her utterances.

He could see it all now. She no longer felt it necessary to behave circumspectly with him. She had taught him the ways of the world, and, as far as she was concerned, that was the end of it.

'Isn't it a little late in the day, sonny boy, for all these scruples? You surely didn't imagine that I had private means!'

Threateningly, he shouted, 'Shut up!'

But instead of shutting her up, he merely goaded her to further excesses, for he had wounded her to the quick.

'No, I will not shut up. On the contrary, I'm going to speak my mind for once. Do you know what I think? I think that, to go to the root of the matter, you deserve no better than that sickly wife of yours.'

'Shut up!' he repeated, with clenched fists.

But she still had more to say. It was horrible. In the end, he was driven to grab her by the wrists and send her flying across the divan.

In spite of all appearances, he knew what he was about. He had had time to decide where he stood. He was fully aware of the consequences of his actions.

It was over.

Over with the League. Over with her. Over with. . . .

Holding himself erect, he went down the stairs, while she stood on the landing, her dressing gown flapping open, yelling insults after him.

From now on, he was all on his own.

VIII

It was as if he had plunged headlong into a tunnel, without a backward glance, without a twinge of regret. He had no idea what lay at the end of it. He no longer even speculated. All he knew was that, sooner or later, he would reach the end of it.

By midday he was still wandering the streets, looking nowhere, seeing nothing. He could still have gone back to the League. It would have been easy. He had made no definite break.

But, in his heart, he knew it was too late. The line was cut. As he had intended that morning, he bought cheese. He even remembered the Roquefort. On his return to the hotel, he asked, 'Have there been any callers for me?'

It had never before occurred to him to ask. Who in the world would think of visiting him? Neither his mother nor his parents-in-law were the sort of people to undertake a journey on impulse, and they would not dream of coming to Paris without prior warning.

Perhaps it was the police he had in mind? But the possibility of a visit from them caused him no anxiety.

No matter what happened, he was ready for anything. Something, now, was bound to happen, and, as far as he was concerned, the sooner the better.

He would even have welcomed the reply, 'There have been developments upstairs . . . . Your wife. . . .'

But everything was perfectly normal. His wife, who was

a lot better, had done the housework. The little bedside table was laid for their meal. It was she who asked, 'You're not feeling too tired, I hope?'

He replied that he was not. It was not fatigue exactly that he was feeling. It was something different, more far-reaching, more deep-seated.

He ate his meal. He left at the usual time, as if bound for the League. He walked and walked, but this time keeping to his own district.

He was in the tunnel, not a dark tunnel, but one shimmering with spring sunshine, to which he had not given a thought since the previous night. He could picture the streets, full of flowers and open cars, crowded terraces and bright dresses.

With the little money still left in his pocket, he could keep going for two days, three at most, not more. He owed money everywhere. There were certain foodshops he avoided, for fear of being seen through the window.

He had lost the will to rebel. All alone among the crowds, he pondered.

Most of the time, he was miles away.

It was not in the least painful. It was almost soothing. God knows why, but he still clung to his hope. Any minute now, Linette might go into labour. Had not Mademoiselle Berthe remarked that in Paris . . . ?

Why should he suppose that this would change anything? He had no idea, but he was convinced that the birth of a child would solve all their problems. At any rate, it would be a sort of sign.

What sort of sign? It was not something that could be expressed in words. A sign from heaven, one might say, a symbol of reconciliation. After all, was it not written in the Bible that the rainbow . . . ?

He returned to the hotel for dinner, just as if he had come back from the League, but said nothing. He was in bed early, to make up for last night's lack of sleep.

When he woke, he found himself back in his tunnel. He went out to his usual bar for his breakfast croissant. In order to save money, he had only one, instead of the five or six he had occasionally indulged in formerly.

People thought they knew him. All of them! Everyone had always imagined they knew him, even the teachers at school, who were wont to look at him with an air of understanding.

It was the same with his mother, and Linette. It was the way of women to imagine that they understood everything, just because they could spot at a glance any small weakness or signs of cowardice in a man.

And the Major . . . he had made his assessment by analogy. He had known others, young like him, eager like him, timid like him, and because they had done this or that, he had concluded that they would all conform to the same pattern.

There was one easy way out. Scarcely even humiliating. All he had to do was to return to the League, go upstairs to the Major's office, and make a confession.

He knew, all too well, how to proceed. Beginning with his wife, needless to say, and the baby whose birth was imminent from one hour to the next . . . . Then he would have to spell out very plainly why it was out of the question to seek help from his family, seeing that it was absolutely essential, for fear of the gravest consequences, that they should remain in ignorance of the fact that he and Linette had been lovers before their marriage.

'Her father would never survive the shame . . . . If you knew him. . . .'

He was perfectly capable of putting his case with great eloquence and sincerity, and finally bursting into tears.

And then the rest: that he was not equipped for life in Paris, that he had at last come to realize this, that the Major had felt it to be so. . . .

That he deserved to be locked up in a lunatic asylum.

That he had been on the brink of going under, in the matter of the petty cash for instance. . . .

Perfect! The Major would be thrilled to bits. He would be deeply moved.

'All I ask is the means of starting life afresh, a different, simpler life, on a much more modest scale, the sort of life I'm really fitted for . . . . Given the chance of finding a job, any job, in a small provincial town, other than Poitiers, I give you my word I'll be able to pay you back in regular monthly instalments.'

There! That was one way out. Another was Monsieur Duhour.

'If you don't help me, I'll blow my brains out.'

He was capable of carrying out his threat, capable at least of contemplating it, providing that, at the eleventh hour . . . Duhour would not believe him. He was a tougher proposition than the Major. And besides, Pilar would no doubt have told him. . . .

Vannier? Perhaps. He might go to Vannier in the end, as a last resort. He would say: 'I've given up the struggle.'

It was the truth in a nutshell. He had given up. But this time, not because he felt discouraged or even despairing, whatever others might think.

Had he ever known anyone capable of understanding him? He walked. Occasionally, he sat down on a bench. He returned often to the Avenue du Bois, idly watching the men and women on horseback, and the cars. He did not feel the slightest touch of envy, they simply did not interest him.

It was another world, very far off, a world with which he had no contact whatsoever.

Linette was still dreaming of her new winter coat. She delighted in going out, to peer in at the windows of the various furriers. Now, she was hesitating between squirrel and beaver.

Well, perhaps! Why not, after all? He read carefully

through all the 'Situations Vacant' columns of the evening newspapers. But he did not put himself forward. He did not apply in writing. He was still waiting for the sign.

It seemed to him that this was something owed to him. He had always done everything humanly possible to help himself. Now it was the turn of Fate to come to his rescue.

He was prepared, that was what mattered.

Prepared to submit. To submit to rules which he did not believe in, but to submit all the same, cheerfully, without revulsion, without bitterness, because it was necessary, because that was what he had come into the world to do.

He was prepared to carry out his duties, day in and day out, to do his best, prepared even to take a certain pride in it, to come home in the evening with a spring in his step, to take his key from his pocket, and cheerfully insert it in the lock.

He was prepared to rock the baby's cradle at night, to wash his feet in a basin until they could afford a bathroom, prepared to dress up in his best suit on Sundays, and wheel the baby's pram, glancing from time to time at the passers-by in their Sunday best.

But at the beginning, no doubt, there would be hardships to be endured. Money! It always came down to that! But surely everything must come right in the end? Was it conceivable that they would be left to die of hunger, here in the heart of Paris, and with a baby on the way?

Once he had reached the decision that he would do everything within his power!

Everything! Including, if need be, if all else failed, going to see his parents-in-law in Poitiers, and confessing the truth to them. His father-in-law would not die of the shock. That was just a fancy of Linette's. There would be tears and reproaches. And then what?

'I promise you that from now on . . .'

And the light in the tunnel was growing brighter all the time. On his way home he smiled, thinking of Linette busily knitting those little pink garments, making her artless little plans. He smiled as he counted his few remaining coins, which would enable him to buy cheese for their evening meal.

'Everything still all right at the League?'

It was no longer for his own sake that he lied to her, but for hers. He said yes, and changed the subject.

He ran into Pilar in the street, on her way to Le Florida. They were still some distance apart. She looked at him hesitantly. He realized that he had only to take a step towards her, to say a word of greeting, and it would start all over again. She missed him, no doubt about it. She looked at him questioningly, almost pleadingly, but he simply walked on more briskly. She, for her part, merely shrugged.

He didn't give a damn what she thought!

He knew what he was about.

Another evening, another night. Something must be done. No doubt Vannier . . . or the Major . . . . He would leave it till the last minute to decide.

If only. . . .

And lo and behold! as he entered the hotel, there was the proprietress, looking thoroughly cross, not to say furious.

'You might have warned me that it was due so soon! Then, at least, we could have arranged to send her to hospital!'

Suddenly, everything seemed bathed in light. Leaving the tunnel behind, he mounted the stairs, two at a time. It seemed to him that he had leapt up them in a single bound. He opened the door, and crashed into a woman in white with straggly grey hair, whom he had never seen before.

'Linette . . .'

The doctor was washing his hands. Linette, chalk-white, with her hair clinging to her forehead, was looking fixedly at him.

Had he seen her lips move? He was not sure of having made out the words, but he could hear them ringing in his head.

'It's a girl.'

All the better. He didn't know why it was all the better, only that it was.

He was torn between laughter and tears. It was over. He was all too well aware that it was all over, that nothing lay ahead of him now but an endless, gentle, downward slope.

He did not go to his wife, nor did he approach the child.

He went and sat in a far corner of the room, leaned with his forearms against the wall, and remained there, all alone, laughing and crying at once.

You see, mother dear, I've been thinking. It wouldn't be right to bring up the baby we are expecting in the stuffy air of Paris. Jean Sabin has behaved very decently, and found me a job on a Corrèze newspaper in Tulle. It's a pretty little town, not at all noisy, and the climate is very healthy. I'm chief reporter on local affairs, and I'm sure it won't be long before I'm entrusted with more important matters. We have found a nice, clean little house with a garden. I know Linette's father will be especially pleased about that. . . .

It was still necessary to distort the facts a little *for them*. But it was almost all true, and it would all be true in time.

He was writing his letter at a table in the brasserie, not far from a group of card players, among them a magistrate. In time, he would be invited to join them. Already, he had reason to be pleased with himself. Only the night before, he had completed a short article for the paper, and signed it with his initials, and on the bench beside him the sun had cast a reassuring reflection.

WGRL-HQ FIC
31057000053374
FIC SIMEN
Simenon, Georges,
The couple from Poitiers